# THE BUN ALSO RISES

BOOK 3: ANGIE PROUTY NANTUCKET COZY
MYSTERY SERIES

## MIRANDA SWEET

HIDDEN KEY PUBLISHING

"All the motives for murder are covered by four Ls: Love, Lust, Lucre and Loathing."

— P.D. James, The Murder Room

# Chapter 1

# THE SAILBOAT

In the dark before the dawn, Angie got up, showered, made coffee, drove to her best friend Jo's apartment, banged on the door, and then let herself in with her copy of the key. Jo was still asleep, open-mouthed and drooling. Her spiky green mohawk had fallen completely flat.

Angie shook Jo's shoulder and stepped back out of the way. They had been friends for a long time, and Angie knew what invariably came next.

Jo flopped over, her outstretched hand slapping the alarm hard enough to knock it against the wall, even though it wasn't ringing. "Five more minutes."

"You're the one who desperately wanted to go kayaking this morning. 'Don't let me sleep in,' you said."

Jo buried her face in her pillow. "Five minutes."

"Aren't you a baker? Don't you normally get up at three a.m. or something? It's four-thirty a.m. You're practically sleeping in."

Jo muttered something into her pillow that sounded suspiciously like cursing.

"Hmm...hung over, are we?" Angie asked slyly, then quickly dodged a pillow that flew at her from across the room.

Laughing, she said, "Coffee's in the living room. In five minutes, I start drinking it. If you want some, you'll have to hurry."

"Don't you dare!" Jo was serious about her caffeine.

Angie gave Jo a wave, closing the door behind her. "Five minutes!"

Twenty minutes later they were climbing into a pair of touring kayaks. The sun was just beginning to rise and the breeze was stiff. The water slapped against the sides of the kayaks as Angie checked over her gear one last time.

Normally, Angie wasn't a big kayaking enthusiast. In fact, she'd always blown it off as something only sporty people did. She was a bookworm and had always been a bookworm. Now, as the owner of a small bookstore, Pastries & Page-Turners, she had all the excuses she would ever need avoid things like jogging, working out at a gym, playing team sports, or kayaking.

But lately she'd been feeling the need to get out and do something. She'd started taking bike rides around the island for fun, playing volleyball with Jo and her twin brother, Mickey, and she'd even purchased a pair of running shoes online. She was just waiting for them to be delivered.

When she'd announced Jo's plan to go kayaking before dawn, Aunt Margery (really her great-aunt, but try calling her that in public), had looked knowingly at Angie.

"Time for a little exercise? 'Everyone thinks of changing the world. No one thinks of changing himself.'"

Aunt Margery had a habit of speaking in literary quotations. Angie was familiar with most of her favorites, but she came up dry on that one. She shook her head.

"Leo Tolstoy," her aunt had finished smugly.

Angie stuck out her tongue. "'Those who cannot change their minds cannot change anything.'"

"George Bernard Shaw," her great-aunt said. Trying to catch her off-guard on a quote was nearly impossible. "Have a good time, dear."

"We should be back by the time the bookstore opens."

"You have an assistant now, one who comes in at the same time you do in the mornings and who, I promise you, will not burn down your bookstore while you're out. And you already told her that she was opening by herself this morning."

Angie took a deep breath and spoke her new mantra to herself: *I will trust my assistant. I will trust my assistant.* Janet Hennery wanted to be a graphic designer and was working at Pastries & Page-Turners to pay the bills. Angie was letting her do all the store's ads in her free time, and their online sales had gone up already. Janet had redesigned the website to make it easier to order books online and business was booming.

On the café side, she also liked to put cute foam pictures on the in-store lattes. She had come up with a new one: an elephant. It was getting so none of the regulars wanted Angie to make their fancy coffees anymore, only Janet.

Angie was fine with that, and she told herself so at least a dozen times a day: *I will trust my assistant.*

Jo pushed her kayak backward with her paddle and slid into the water. The streetlights over the beach were still lit, but the sky to the east was taking on a gorgeous purplish hue. Angie and Jo were in for a beautiful sunrise.

"I know what you're thinking," Jo said. "You're saying that stupid mantra again, aren't you? About trusting your assistant and not freaking out about leaving the store with her."

"Maybe," Angie said, then stuck her tongue out.

Jo paused, digging her paddle into the sand as the water lapped against the side of the white-and-green kayak. "You ready to go?"

"Yep," Angie said with a nod. "I have my phone in a waterproof bag and ready to speed-dial 911 at the slightest sign of sharks or storms. I have sunscreen, sandwiches, and a thermos full of espresso shots. I have—"

Jo interrupted. "We have espresso shots. What else do we need? Let's go!"

They shoved off into the water and started paddling. The plan was to circle around the Brant Point Lighthouse, past Jetties Beach, out around the ruins of the old lighthouse on Whale Rock, and then all the way to Washing Pond Beach where they would stop for breakfast. It was about four miles each way.

The water slid around the kayak, making soft popping and gulping sounds as the vessel negotiated the peaks and valleys of the waves.

They passed the Brant Point lighthouse, looking squat and white and smug against the sand. A fisherman gave them a cheery hello. Jo stopped just past the point, raising a hand to tell Angie to stop paddling. A forty-foot #1 Hull charter boat was exiting the harbor. Several faces smiled at them from the railing. Jo made Angie turn the nose of her kayak at a right angle to the ferry's wake, and they bounced up and down for a couple of moments.

"Too much?" Jo asked. "You aren't seasick or anything, are you?" Sometimes it was like Jo was her second mom.

Angie had been grinning. "No, I'm fine."

"Let's get out of the harbor."

They kayaked past Jetties Beach.

"You're not getting tired, are you?"

"No, I'm fine."

The sun was now up. A pretty, multi-sailed friendship sloop, a smallish type of sailboat, was anchored along the coast. The sails were a gorgeous red color. Several other boats were nearby and buoys had been set up to create a boundary.

"Someone must be getting sailing lessons," Angie said. "We should go around."

"Just keep an eye out for passing boats," Jo said. "They can run over us faster than we can get out of the way."

Angie felt a hint of nervousness as they began making their way around the buoys. The strong current was making it difficult to move forward. She was working hard, and the muscles in her lower back ached.

"Hey," Jo called back over her shoulder, "next weekend, should we go to the movies? I think that one with the guy you like is coming out soon."

"*Or* we could go to a play in Boston," Angie, who would rather see films at home in her PJs while curled up with a glass of red wine, said.

"Look, I can only take so much high culture a month. Let's go to some punk shows."

"Only if you buy me a pair of steel-toe boots first," Angie replied. "I thought I was going to break a toe last time." Jo had dragged her into the mosh pit and someone had stepped on her feet and she had fallen. This had been in high school almost twenty years ago, but neither one would let the other forget about it.

On the other side of the buoys, the sloop started moving. The mainsail dipped as it unfurled, catching the wind. The sailboat rushed toward the shore, turning away at the last minute. It flew alongside the boundary marked by the buoys and rushed toward the shore again.

"What are they doing?" Angie wondered aloud.

"Dunno." Jo had taken out her phone and was recording the boats.

Angie stretched upward in her seat. "Why aren't they turning this time?"

The sloop seemed to be headed straight for Whale Rock.

Angie dropped the paddle across the kayak and put her hands over her mouth. She could barely breathe.

Jo was still recording.

It was too late for the boat to turn. The rocks under the waves made the sailboat jerk as they caught against the keel. The current pulled the boat sideways, turning it sharply.

The bowsprit, the long piece of wood jutting out in front of the boat, turned directly toward Whale Rock.

The smaller boats that had been around the sloop finally noticed what was happening and were rushing toward it. Two figures were moving along the deck of the sloop, frantically trying to adjust the ropes.

"Oh no," Angie whispered.

The sloop slammed into the ruins of the lighthouse; the two men dove off the stern into the water.

The bowsprit shattered against the lighthouse base, the sails crumpling as the tension went out of them.

"Jo! Jo! We have to help them! We need to get over there!"

"I think they have it under control," Jo said, eerily calm.

The boats on either side seemed to be hanging back and the two men were swimming through the choppy surf near the rocks.

"But they could get hurt!"

The swimmers made it away from the wreckage, then turned back to it, treading water.

The sloop's keel, now almost completely clear of the water, began to tip and fall. The mast and sails sank into the water.

The two men, finally realizing their danger, tried to swim away but the current was pushing the wreckage toward them, faster than they could escape.

The stern swept over one of the men, dragging him under. The other had managed to swim further away but was hit by the boat, going under briefly, then bobbing up.

Angie's heart was in her throat. On the other side of the sloop, the second man surfaced again, struggling with one of the sails.

"Call 911," she told Jo. "Oh my God. You have to call 911."

Jo didn't answer.

Angie shook her head back and forth, as if by sheer willpower alone, she could tell the fates to undo what she had just seen. She was sick to her stomach.

Suddenly, a siren blasted three times, and the two boats that had been hanging back from the wreckage rushed toward the men in the water. Within moments, a pair of life preservers had been cast and the two figures were being pulled onto a boat.

A hush seemed to hang over the area. Then, in the distance, Angie heard a cheer go up.

"They're okay, they're okay!" she said.

Jo recorded a few more seconds, then lowered the phone, giving Angie a huge grin. "Just remember that I have *every word* you just said on this recording, which I am already uploading online."

"What are you talking about?" Angie asked.

Several other boats moved in toward Whale Rock, throwing out lines to pull the wreckage away from the rocks.

"We just watched a movie being filmed and those were stuntmen! You were *totally* freaking out! You are a*dork*able."

"A...movie?" There was no movie being filmed on Nantucket! She would have heard about it by now if there were.

"Yeah, a movie," Jo said. She began paddling her way toward the beach, cutting inside the line of buoys.

Angie had a sudden urge to smack her friend in the head with a kayak paddle. "You let me freak out on purpose!"

Jo's evil laugh echoed back to her across the waves.

# Chapter 2

# THE BREAKFAST COUP

As it turned out, they did *not* have breakfast on Washing Pond Beach. After about five minutes of hard paddling, Jo let herself drift to a stop. Angie pulled up alongside her. Jo was still giggling. She stopped to wipe the tears off her face with the back of her hand.

"Thank you for not killing me," she said.

"A movie?" Angie said incredulously.

"Yeah. A Hallmark special, so, you know. No A-lister Hollywood stars or anything. Teddy told me about it. He has a friend who's working as a gaffer, you know, one of the electricians working behind the scenes. Top secret. I had to promise that I wouldn't tell anyone."

Angie rolled her eyes. Teddy was Jo's punk-rock boyfriend from the mainland. "Obviously you didn't tell anyone. Including me."

Jo chuckled, clearly pleased with herself.

The boats were headed back toward the jetty. The boat hauling the sloop's wreckage was moving along at a much slower pace.

"Ready for breakfast?" Jo said.

"Breakfast," she said, a thought forming in her mind. She turned toward Jo. "Where are *they* going for breakfast?"

"I dunno, wherever."

Angie leaned toward her best friend and said, "If you do not call Teddy's friend and invite the crew out to Pastries and Page-Turners for coffee and breakfast, I really will kill you. *You owe me for doing this to me.*"

Jo called Teddy, and the two women turned around and rushed back to Jetties Beach, where Angie hitched a ride back to the bookstore. Janet had just opened and was serving a group of regulars, mostly retirees, who queued up each day for their early morning coffee.

Checking the fridges, Angie announced, "We're gonna be swamped in about fifteen minutes." They were about to run out of milk. "I'll be right back." She drove to the store and picked up six gallons of two percent, got in line at the checkout, then went back for a variety of vegan milk—soy, almond, and rice.

The manager at the cash register said, "Something going on at the bookshop?"

"Tell you later." Angie wasn't sure if she was held to Jo's promise of secrecy. She waved as she pushed the cart out to her car.

She was thinking, *Walter had to have known about the movie.* Walter was her very recent ex-boyfriend who had vowed to remain her *friend*. The Chamber of Commerce would have had to know about the movie filming, and he was one of their biggest supporters. *And he didn't tell me.*

As she pulled into the bookstore parking lot, a series of restored VW

Microbuses rolled around the corner behind her. They often ran large groups of tourists around the island. They must have been hired for the film crew. She ran inside with as much of the milk as she could carry, left it on the back counter, and ran for the wheeled cart she used to haul books around. The front door was already jingling.

Soon she was on the register while Janet was making lattes as fast as she could. "Skim? Skim?!" Janet called out.

"I forgot to buy skim," Angie groaned. She grabbed a sheet of printer paper, wrote, "OUT OF SKIM – SOY, ALMOND, RICE, COW 2% ONLY," and gave it to one of the people in line to stick it on the front door for her.

Almost before the line for coffee had been settled, the line for buying books began. Local history books flew off the shelves, as well as bestsellers that had recently been turned into movies. One hardy soul, a tall, scruffy-cheeked man wearing a backward Red Sox hat, walked up to the counter with a stack of about a dozen old, used best-selling paperbacks from the racks in the front—basically, the books that Angie left for the regulars to read and argue over in the mornings.

"I want these," he said. "All of these."

The other people from the set of the movie had mostly bought new paperbacks and hardcovers. She sized him up. His sneakers, blue jeans, and sweatshirt, with the CRI Community Rowing Club logo, were worn but not cheap.

"Are you going to read them all?" she asked.

With an almost completely straight face, he said, "Yes. And then I'm going to bring them back and get some more. I'm a reader."

She tried to suppress a smile. "Hi, reader. I'm Angie. I'm also a reader."

"That's good. I'd hate to think of a bookstore owner not being a reader." He held out his hand.

She shook it. "Haven't you read *any* of these?"

He shrugged. "For the most part, yes. But I don't have a lot of free time to be away from the set. I'm the director of photography. I just grabbed the ones up front because I gotta go."

He must have been on one of those boats this morning!

"Which ones haven't you read?"

He pulled out three, setting them carefully, corners aligned, on the counter, separate from the others.

She leaned forward. "If you give me your email, I'll send you a list of titles that you might not have read but that you might like. You tell me which ones you want, and I'll deliver them and pick up whatever you're done with."

He lifted one eyebrow. "You'd do that?"

Angie smiled. "Coffee. Pastries. Book delivery by bicycle, we do it all."

His face lit up. "That's just about the greatest thing I've ever heard."

"I'll start an account for you. The fees for the books you bring back will come out of the price for the next set of books."

"I don't even care about that. I just want someone to bring me books. My eyes get tired of reading from my phone," he added. "I have to do print."

"I understand." She got his information—his name was Al Petrillo and he lived in L.A., but was, he explained, originally from Boston. He walked over to the café tables and sat down, stopping only to give a satisfied wave to Angie before he dove into one of his books.

"You've made a friend for life," said the next person in line, a woman so beautiful that Angie knew she had to be one of the stars of the movie. Which, come to think of it, she didn't even know the name of. She had a book in her hand, something on the French film director Robert Bresson. "Al's a total book nut."

Along with the book, the woman ordered a cup of coffee, black with no cream, then said, "What's your favorite type of cupcake? Gimme one of those."

Angie looked over at what was still in the case. "They're all really good, but what you really want is for me to pick one out because they look too good to choose just one, right? How about a mincemeat cupcake?"

"Mincemeat?" the woman said as her eyebrows skewed with uncertainty. "That sounds weird, but kind of hip. Sure, I'll give it a shot."

Angie rang her up and asked, "What's your role in the movie? Can you tell me the name of the movie? I've been dying of curiosity all morning, by the way."

The woman lifted one expressive eyebrow. "My role? I don't have one. I'm the makeup artist. Sandra Potvin."

Sandra had tattoos up and down both arms. Angie caught a glimpse of angel wings, clocks, and – most notably – what looked like a small beaker. They were some of the most gorgeous tattoos that Angie had ever seen, delicately tinted and etched into the woman's skin. There were even a few tattoos that crept out of the neck of the woman's loose, sleeveless gray t-shirt. The t-shirt itself seemed tattooed with line art depicting a heart pierced by three swords. It was a tarot reference; Angie struggled to remember what it meant.

"You're beautiful enough to be the star," Angie told her.

Ms. Potvin smiled and rolled her eyes at the same time. "Thank you. But this is a Hallmark movie, so my elaborate body art isn't exactly on-brand."

"That's too bad, those are really beautiful." As Angie gestured toward the tattoos on Sandra's arm.

Ms. Potvin gave her a quick smile.

As Angie was getting her coffee a woman in a business suit came through the door. The rest of the crew members weren't dressed in business office attire; they were far more casual. But, several of the crew members greeted the woman, who was talking on her phone as she walked toward the counter.

Reaching the counter, the woman moved the phone from her lips and ordered a skim milk latte with six shots of espresso.

"I'm sorry, we're out of skim," Angie said.

"One moment," she said into the phone, as she lifted her chin. "What do you have, then?"

"Two percent cow, almond, soy, rice."

"Why didn't you put up a sign or something?"

Angie resisted the urge to retort sarcastically that she had.

After a long pause, the woman said, "Soy. No whip," and went back to the conversation on her phone, handing Angie a credit card.

"Soy latte, six shots, no whip," Angie told Janet.

"But we don't normally put whip on..." Janet leaned over to get a look at the customer who wanted six shots of espresso, making a whistling sound at the sight of the stern-faced woman in a professionally tailored suit talking on the phone. "Never mind. Got it, boss."

The name on the credit card read *Lucy Smith*. The woman was pretty, but definitely not charming enough to be a movie star. She just didn't have that kind of magnetism. Sandra Potvin did though. And despite being a makeup artist, Sandra wasn't wearing much of the stuff—just some eyeliner and lip gloss.

A thin, short man came into the bookstore wearing a polo shirt, khakis, and a pair of scuffed brown dress shoes. Everyone's eyes turned toward him. It was suddenly quiet.

He scurried up to Ms. Smith. "Aren't you ready yet?" It wasn't an authoritative, pushy question; it was said with almost a hint of despair.

"I'm getting a latte."

"He's not here yet is he?" Ms. Smith asked carefully.

"Not yet."

Ms. Smith's shoulders relaxed slightly. The tension in the room seemed to drop a little.

Whoever "he" was, was someone to be dreaded, apparently.

"I need that latte," Ms. Smith announced to Janet.

"Two more shots."

"Just give it to me. I need to leave."

Janet poured in the second pair of shots, then handed the latte over the counter, adding a second paper cup to help insulate the first. Angie had asked her to use the paper sleeves instead of extra cups, which was less wasteful—but she immediately knew, as Janet must have, that Ms. Smith would complain about having to use a sleeve. Maybe today was just a bad day for her.

Ms. Smith accepted the latte and she and the new guy left without another word.

Sandra returned to the counter, handing over her empty mug for a refill. She said, "The *look* on your face."

"I hope I wasn't rude."

"Don't worry about it. That's probably how they think people normally look. They're assistants. Lucy Smith works for the female lead, Julia Withers, and Lloyd Rapinski works for the producer, Lance Mitchell. Hopefully you'll never meet him. He's an awful human being."

"Why?"

"Where do I start? First, he's brilliant. Second, he never lets you forget it, and third, he has no regard for anyone's feelings," Sandra said drily. "He's famous for writing a book on French film *auteurs* – which is just his really obnoxious way of letting you know he can say 'director' in French - and he never lets you forget it. In short, he's a major jerk."

"Oh?"

"He's the kind of guy you regret ever having met," Sandra said, shaking her head to herself and walking away.

She watched Sandra walk off and glanced over at the man she'd met earlier - Al Petrillo. She sighed. Angie felt a pang of heartache and a touch of anger brewing as she saw that backward Red Sox hat.

Walter was a Red Sox fan.

Angie had thought things with Walter were going okay. They had gotten through the awkward phase of dating and had slid into a comfortable routine. Walter was tall, dark, and handsome. He was funny, and his heart was in the right place. Like herself, he was a bookworm. He was even rich, by far the richest man on the island.

However, Angie sensed something had gone wrong, although she couldn't quite place what it was. The passion she had felt when they first met had been muted by distance. Walter was on and off island constantly for work, and even though Boston was only a 45-minute flight from Nantucket, Angie felt the distance.

She and Walter got along well, but their phone conversations had grown so... friendly. Despite this, Angie had told herself things were going fine.

Nearly two months ago, Walter had invited her to the newest restaurant on the island, a place called Nonatum's Food and Beverage, on Nonatum Avenue and Surfside Road. The restaurant had a wraparound porch with amazing views of the water, and was supposed to be great as a romantic, fine dining location.

But the owners were in a feud with another local business, Sheldon's Shuckery - an oyster bar with more character than a Shakespearian comedy. It was practically an island institution. Nonatum's owner had said something snide about the Shuckery in an interview in the *Boston Herald*'s Lifestyle section, and gossip was flying all over the island. That kind of bad-mouthing simply was not done by Nantucket locals. The new restaurant had earned a lot of ill-will from the locals over one simple comment, and now it was struggling for business. Just because the Shuckery's owners hadn't gone to a famous cooking school didn't mean it wasn't one of the finest dining experiences on the island. Anyone who loved food ate at Sheldon's. Angie couldn't help but think that perhaps Nonatum's owner was just jealous.

The co-owner of the Shuckery, Sheldon's French wife, Jeanette, was a firm believer that a couple of pounds of butter and cheese never hurt anybody. Eating at Sheldon's was good for the soul, but maybe not for your cholesterol.

As a local business owner, Angie was squarely aligned with Sheldon's. Angie had gone on the date feeling uncomfortable. Should she say something about the bad blood between Nonatum and Sheldon's? Was Walter just bringing her along as some kind of political move? As one of the major and most powerful property owners on the island, he was always trying to keep business on the island smooth and prosperous.

Or was this nothing more than a regular date? Maybe, she thought, she was overthinking things. Just a little.

Nonatum's was in a big gray shake-shingle-sided building that glowed in the sunset. The air was chilly, and Angie, who had dumped her usual waterproof jacket for a fancier, much lighter ivory sweater, was shivering as she walked through the front door.

The fancy looking menu seemed to offer at least one dish from each of the latest food trends, but it was nothing like the mouthwatering foods offered at the Shuckery.

Their waitress appeared stressed and hurried, and it took forever to get their food. When it arrived, it was fine. Not worth what Walter was paying for it, but fine.

Angie smiled at Walter, and he gave her a grim nod back. Angie had a bad feeling in the pit of her stomach.

After having paid the check, Walter seemed to interrupt her thoughts. "Walk along the beach," he asked, "to help us digest?"

Out on the cold sand Walter stopped, with the wind blowing off the ocean and the reflection of the moon glittering on the waves. He slowly turned to Angie and said, "I'm sorry. I tried to think of a way to tell you before we got to the restaurant, but I couldn't do it."

"What is it?"

"This isn't working out," he said. "I think we should see other people."

She turned away from him, her cheeks flaming. Whether she felt rage, sadness, or a combination of the two, Angie wasn't sure.

"Angie... What are you thinking?" Walter's brows were furrowed together.

"I don't know what to say. I've been having similar feelings, but I didn't think it was going to end this soon, either. Or that *you'd* want to end it." After an awkward pause she added, "Why now?"

Walter shifted uneasily.

"There's someone else, isn't there?" Angie asked, growing angrier by the moment.

"No. No, not like that," he said. "There's somebody at work, but nothing has happened. I don't know Angie, I just think it's time for us to move on."

"Wait...*what?*! There's someone *else*? Who is she?" Angie exclaimed, with pure fire in her voice.

"A lawyer friend from Boston."

"Are you kidding me, Walter? You're just going to drop this on me?" Angie couldn't believe it. Sure, the passion they had once shared may or may not have died down, but she was shocked there was another woman in the picture.

Angie wanted to cry and scream at the same time.

"I can't believe this, Walter. The nerve you have taking me to dinner and then telling me this! Another woman!" Angie practically spat her words out.

"Angie, I told you, nothing has happened yet, I wouldn't do that to you. I'm so sorry," He replied, taking a step back and biting his lip.

They stood for a moment, saying nothing. Angie noticed Walter was shivering. He'd been standing between her and the wind. *Good, let him freeze,* thought Angie. She turned to walk away from him, deciding she'd rather face the blustery weather than continue this conversation.

As she headed back to the restaurant's parking lot, Walter struggled to catch up with her. He broke the silence. "Uh, Angie...I just want you to know that the only reason we're at Nonatum's is that I didn't want to take you to Sheldon's to end things," he admitted. "I mean... Sheldon's is a place for happy memories, you know? I wouldn't want you to start avoiding Shelly's over something between us."

Angie bitterly laughed. *Wow,* she thought, *how considerate.*

They reached Walter's car and he opened the door for her. She glared at him and got in. They drove back to Angie's house in silence.

"Will you be all right?" he asked as he pulled into her driveway.

Angie opened the car door. "I'll be just fine," she said, stepping out. The door slammed behind her.

Walter rolled down the passenger window and called out to Angie. "You'll still sell me books though, right?"

She gave him a curt smile. "Sure, Walter. We've got a whole breakup book section that I'd be happy to show you."

Walter seemed to take this comment in stride, pausing only to briefly nod before he drove off.

Angie had known in her heart that she and Walter were not meant to be, and she tried to console herself with the knowledge that she would move on. Her anger would help her get through this.

But it still hurt.

Following the breakup, Jo, of course, had told her that Walter didn't deserve her and that she would gladly spray-paint curse words on the side of his mansion out on Polpis Road, if it would make Angie feel better. Her twin brother Mickey had said he was creating a commemorative dessert to cheer Angie up from the whole thing, but then brought over a box of his regular cupcakes, which were excellent but hardly honoring the situation.

"You're going to make me fat," Angie said.

Mickey was over six feet tall and still a beanpole, despite being a baker. He chortled and rubbed his hands together. "I'm going to make everyone fat!"

"You should have at least made a different dessert if you were making a commemorative dessert."

He nodded. "Now that I think about it, a cupcake doesn't properly reflect the gravity of the situation...*or does it?*"

She rolled her eyes.

"Well, at least now you can solve all the mysteries on the island in peace," Mickey said.

She sneered at him.

"You know, if someone gets murdered again," he said as a mischievous smile split his face in half, "or man-slaughtered or whatever."

"What? No. Mickey, come on." Her stomach lurched. She had always been self-conscious about her sleuthing. "I refuse to get mixed up with that kind of thing anymore."

He leaned over the coffee table and dropped the cupcakes on top of a stack of oversized books. "You cannot refuse," he said in a deep, spooky voice. "It *ees* in your *blood*."

Angie put her hands over her face. "Please, Mickey. Just stop."

"Fine." he said, suddenly backing off. "Forget I said anything. Anyways, don't eat all the cupcakes at once. I made a new kind."

"What?" she said from between her fingers.

Mickey paused for a second. Then he said, "Oh, uh, mincemeat."

"*Mincemeat?*" she asked.

"Try it. You'll like it," he said as he stepped out the door.

The cupcake itself was made of gingerbread cake, the topping was cream cheese frosting, and the center was a raisin-and-apple filling, slightly spicy. After the first bite, Angie stopped and heated up some apple cider to go with it, then decided to take a walk along the street. It had just rained, and the cobbles were wet. She could see the tracks from Mickey's car in the driveway.

The bell over the bookstore door rang, snapping Angie out of her reverie. It was Mickey Jerritt.

Mickey glanced around the room admiringly. "Hey, cool. This place is *packed*. Did you sell anybody my cupcakes? How did you like the mincemeat?"

"Sorry, Mickey. It's been more breakfast pastries than anything else," she said. "I did sell one mincemeat cupcake, though."

"But they're *gourmet* cupcakes," he said, in a slightly raised voice.

"Not everyone wants cupcakes for breakfast."

"Inconceivable," Mickey said loudly.

About six people replied in unison, "I do not think that word means what you think it means." Yeah, they were around a bunch of film geeks now, all right. Practically everyone had *The Princess Bride* memorized.

"But the mincemeat?" he said. "At least tell me what *you* thought about it."

"I warmed up some apple cider and took it outside to eat. It was the perfect fall cupcake."

"Great," he said. "The story of my life. The perfect fall cupcake. In April."

He put his back to the counter and looked over the room. "So, you're not killing my sister for deceiving you this morning, are you? She may still be slightly concerned."

"This morning's business more than makes up for it, honestly," Angie said. "But you don't actually have to tell her that."

"Heh. I'll let her stew for a while."

"Are you here looking for movie stars, too?"

"Nah, I already had a sighting. The female lead and her assistant."

"The assistant's name is Lucy Smith. Six shots of espresso, skim milk."

He frowned at her. "Isn't there a sign on the door saying you're out of skim milk?"

"I got the impression that she might not be the most observant person ever."

"Well, I thought she was pretty. Just kind of stressed, you know?"

"I guess." Angie thought the woman was an unpleasant, stuck-up snob, but she didn't want to argue about it in front of customers. Besides, Mickey would pretend that she was just being jealous. "What was the female lead like?"

"So pretty it was almost surreal," he said. "Like, I literally choked up. I couldn't speak."

"Hot?"

He held out a hand and made a *so-so* gesture. "I guess? Crazy beautiful. But she has that wholesome look, no smolder, you know?"

"And you're looking for *smolder*, is that it, Mickey?" said Angie playfully.

"Yeah, something like that. Smoldering hot, and really into baked goods, that's my kind of woman." Mickey held Angie's eyes for a moment too long.

The door jingled again. Mickey straightened up his tall frame. "Speak of the devil. That's her."

Angie recognized Lucy Smith. The woman with her *was* incredibly pretty, but kind of sweet and innocent looking. Mickey had called it. He ducked around the counter, put his hand softly on Angie's shoulder and grinned. "See you later," he whispered, and disappeared out the back door.

Angie watched him walk out, and then snapped her attention back to the counter. The two women approached her. Janet was taking a break. Angie started pulling a double shot. "Still no skim. Soy okay?"

Ms. Smith's attitude was about a thousand times more pleasant now that her boss was around. "Yes, please." Angie built the second latte and waved away the woman's credit card. Her boss looked around the bookstore with wide blue eyes, the charming expression of an ingenue on her face and her mouth slightly open. "This place! It's so *wonderful!*" said the actress.

"May I get you anything?"

"I would like..." The woman stared at the menu on the hanging chalkboard over the counter; it had been Janet's idea. She had embellished it with colored chalks and decorative lettering. "I would like a spicy chai."

Angie wasn't sure whether the woman was in character or not. If not, she was quite the character all by herself. "Certainly." Angie started making the drink for her.

When she looked up, the woman had disappeared. Angie looked around, then heard purring. She peered over the counter and looked down. The store cat, Captain Parfait, had come out of hiding. He had claimed the movie star as his own private petting machine and was rubbing his face on her hands and legs as the woman talked to him in a baby voice. "Who's a good kitty? Oh, you are the best-est kitty in the whole wide world, aren't you?"

Angie couldn't help but smile. The assistant, Ms. Smith, scowled at Captain Parfait as if to say *Hurt her and I'll kill you.*

Angie decided that the movie star must be sweet and a little naïve. She was just *too* cute. No wonder she was in a Hallmark movie.

Finally, she stood up. Ms. Smith had already paid for the chai on her own credit card. "I just *love* your kitty. What's his name?"

Angie introduced her to Captain Parfait, and then to herself. The star's name was Julia Withers, but she asked to just be called Julia. Angie told her that she was welcome to come to the bookstore whenever they were open to visit the cat, although she warned her that normally Captain Parfait didn't like to be out and about when there were too many customers. He was more of a professional mouser than anything else.

"You have...mice?" Julia asked, as if she couldn't remember exactly what mice were.

"Not often," Angie said. "But it's an old building, from back in the eighteen hundreds, and one mouse is one too many for a bookstore."

"Oh, I'm sure."

"When he can't find real mice, he likes to tear up my bookmarks and leave them on the mat for me to find, and then I have to pet him and praise him for being a good hunter, or he sulks."

Julia laughed. Her face softened a little. Her expression had been slightly strained before, almost unnoticeably so. "Every cat is a complete brat in one way or another, aren't they? That's why I love them. I miss my cat at home. His name is Cookie. If I try to read scripts in front of him, he starts hissing and tries to bite me. He also likes to lick people's armpits. I only sleep with my head sticking out of the covers, but once I woke up because my mother was staying over, and I'd forgotten to warn her. She *screamed* and terrified him. Haha, he deserved it, though!"

They both looked at Captain Parfait, who immediately laid on his side and cocked one leg up in the air, all the better to wash his unmentionables. They both laughed.

"He knows we're just teasing." Julia sighed. "The news is out that we're here by now, I suppose. This is the last day of peace that we'll have all month. I may as well enjoy it. If I take my shoes off and sit on the floor with a book in the back, you won't stress over it too much, will you?"

"Take the kids' nook," Angie suggested. "There's a bean bag and a big stuffed dog. Sit behind the dog and nobody will even know that you're there."

"Thank you," Julia said, and walked off into the stacks in the direction Angie had pointed.

Ms. Smith waited until Julia was far enough away and then turned to Angie.

"I looked you up." She said with a raised eyebrow.

"Oh?" replied Angie.

"You're dating Walter Snuock, the son of the man who you found dead last Fourth of July."

Angie took a step away from the woman. Her face was burning. It was true, but so blunt and so sudden that it shocked her. "They must not have updated the gossip websites yet," she said. "We broke up. Pretty recently."

Ms. Smith nodded as if they'd been having a perfectly normal conversation. "My point is that you know what it's like to be dragged into the spotlight."

*But I'm not an actress,* Angie wanted to say. *I didn't sign up for it.* "I guess I do," she said instead.

"Take that times a thousand. And then imagine trying to work while everyone is watching over your shoulder. Miss Julia has been under a lot of scrutiny lately. The last thing she needs is someone announcing that they have a movie star visiting their little bookstore, and everyone should stop in. This needs to be a safe space for Julia, not a ploy for someone to use her to gain business."

Angie gaped at her. "I would never do something like that. I can't stop the tourists from being, well, tourists, and posting pictures of her all over social media, but I'm not a jerk."

Ms. Smith gave her another nod that said *Now we understand each other.*

"If anyone bothers Julia I'll strangle them myself. I've handled worse," Ms. Smith said.

Weren't personal assistants supposed to be personable? Charming?

Probably it didn't matter, as long as they were well-organized. Angie placed Julia's drink on the counter.

Ms. Smith grabbed her boss's chai. She looked Angie in the eyes and squared her shoulders.

"I'm glad we had time for this little chat. I'll be out of your hair as long as we're on the same page. Julia's not bothered, you're not bothered. Got it?" Without pausing for an answer, Ms. Smith turned on her heel and walked off in search of Julia.

Angie took a deep breath. All in all, it had been a pretty strange morning at the book store. Meeting movie stars, being chewed out by personal assistants... None of this was on Angie's usual list of daily activities at Pastries & Page-Turners.

Irked by the disruption to her normally calm bookstore, Angie decided it was time for a visit to Carol Brightwell at the Chamber of Commerce to find out why she was the last to know about this movie.

After having told Janet she would be stepping out of the store, Angie rounded the corner of the cobblestone street and headed off in the direction of Carol's office. The day had turned out to be absolutely beautiful, with the sun shining down on Angie.

She hurried down the street and found herself in front of the old red building that was the island's Chamber of Commerce. Pushing past the heavy front door, Angie soon found her way to Carol, executive director of the building and self-appointed busybody. If there was a question to be answered on the island, Carol was your woman.

She appeared to be in the midst of an irritating phone call. "Hey, Angie. Give me a minute," Carol said, holding her finger up.

Angie glanced around the office and decided to get settled into a plush blue armchair. No telling how long this could take.

After several minutes of impatient nods and "Uh-huh...Yeah's," Carol was off the phone.

"Sorry about that. We've got some demanding requests coming in for the summer. You know how it goes," Carol said with a wink. "What can I do for you?"

Angie took a deep breath. "Carol, why didn't you tell me there was a movie being filmed on the island? I got harassed by the star's assistant today. I completely freaked out when I witnessed what I thought was a *boat crash* this morning."

"I know, wasn't it exciting?!" Carol seemed practically giddy.

"I thought that two men had been seriously injured. You could have warned me."

"I know, I know. It was a big secret, though. They wanted to film *one particular scene* without a lot of people around to gawk. A sailboat crashing, so dramatic! And just think! You found out about it regardless. It all worked out!"

"How did you know about it if it was supposed to be such a big secret?"

"Jeanette told me. She's such a dear. Apparently, she knows the director, or producer, or something. Oh, listen to me. Like I know all the Hollywood terms!" Carol slapped her knee and giggled, pleased with herself.

"Carol, I'm being serious. I might need you to do crowd control at the bookstore. Julia Withers has a very serious assistant dead set on keeping her out of the spotlight and I don't want to make that woman mad," Angie widened her eyes when she said "serious," hoping that would emphasize Lucy's intimidating ways.

"No problem there. You tell me when you need me! I'm happy to come to the bookstore any time. You want me to head over now?" Carol started to get up from her desk, eagerly rubbing her hands together.

*Ah-ha.* Angie realized that Carol wanted to see a movie star. She was just the kind of person who needed to be kept away from Julia Withers.

"No, it's fine. I'll let you know if I need you," Angie sighed.

"Don't be mad at me, Ang. I can't stand it," Carol paused and looked around dramatically, changing her voice to a whisper. "How about I give you a peek at some *extra special, very secret* information that got dropped by my office yesterday?"

"What is it?" Angie asked carefully.

Carol dug through one of the drawers in her desk and pulled out a thick, wrinkled stack of papers. She slapped it on the desk. "A Nantucket Romance by Hank Seaton" was written on the top page.

"Carol! Is this the movie script?!" Angie couldn't believe it. An actual Hollywood script right in front of her.

"Can I read it? Please?"

Carol nodded with a smile, clearly pleased. "Of course, Angie. It's the beautiful story of a wealthy doctor who comes to Nantucket to hide from life after a painful divorce. He and his best friend suffer a sailboat crash, and they barely survive. While in the hospital, both he and his best friend fall in love with the same woman, their nurse.

True Hollywood magic, happening right here on our little island," Carol stared dreamily into the distance.

"I want to see how this morning's crash fits into the plot, so thank you. This *almost* makes up for you not giving me a head's up but, hey, next time how about keeping your favorite bookstore owner in the loop?" Angie asked.

Carol nodded dutifully and rose from her chair, escorting Angie out to the Chamber of Commerce lobby.

Just as the two women were saying their goodbyes, two men wearing baseball caps entered through the front door. Angie stopped to look at them directly and realized that they could pass for twins. They were both kind of cute, tall and muscular through the shoulders, with baby faces and dimples in their chins. One wore a Detroit Tigers baseball cap that he kept pulled low over his eyes, a rumpled button-up, and jeans; the other wore a New York Yankees baseball jacket and had a fresh black eye – whether this was from a baseball rival-induced argument or what, Angie wasn't sure.

"Are you gentlemen lost?" Carol peered at them, making no point in hiding her admiration of their biceps.

"Well, ma'am, I don't think so. Is this the Chamber of Commerce?" The man in the Detroit cap asked.

"It is. My name is Carol Brightwell and I'm the executive director of this fine building. This is my friend Angie Prouty." Both women exchanged handshakes with the guys. "May I help you two with something?"

Both guys nodded at the same time. It was eerie. They really did look like twins.

"Actually, yes. My friend and I are here to do some work for the movie being filmed. I've absolutely fallen in love with this beautiful little island. I'd love the name of a good realtor," Detroit cap said.

Both Angie and Carol nearly fell over with laughter. A *realtor?* Was this crew guy thinking of buying a house here? Angie wasn't sure how much set members were paid, but she felt terrible imagining what his reaction would be to the cost of a tiny inland cottage.

The two guys raised their eyebrows at the laughter. Detroit hat held a straight face.

"Oh, um... Okay! Come with me! I'm happy to point the way to my favorite Nantucket realtor. She sold me my house," Carol pointed in the direction of her office.

Detroit hat nodded happily and looked over at Angie, offering her a stunning smile. *He looks so familiar,* Angie thought. *And what a great smile.*

"Well, good luck with the house. If you need a coffee or a good book, I'd love to see you at the bookstore," Angie stuck her hand out to the two men.

"Nice to meet you," Yankees hat said with a grin.

"We look forward to getting some java from you in the future," Detroit hat replied.

Angie stepped away from the group, stopping to turn and look at Carol.

"Carol, no more secrets. Okay?" Angie pleaded. The last thing she needed was a *second* movie showing up for filming.

"I'm so sorry, Angie. I promise. No more secrets or surprises. Business as usual!" Carol gave an apologetic smile and proceeded to lead the two men off in search of a realtor.

Chapter 3

# A GOOD SELECTION
# OF BOOKS

The next morning, Angie and Janet both showed up to open the store. It was a Saturday, so even if the movie crew didn't stop by, it was going to be busy.

But the crew did show up. Most of them showed up early, but some of them drifted in and out as the day went on, carried around the island by the VW Microbuses.

It was a slightly different group, although she recognized Al Petrillo (who had read one of the books overnight and took another two with him that she recommended), Sandra Potvin, and a few of the others. The star, Julia Withers, didn't appear, and of the two similar-looking men who had shown up the day before, only the Yankees fan with the shiner was present.

Much to Angie's chagrin, Lucy Smith appeared, ordered the same thing as before, then negotiated to have coffee catered to the movie set for the rest of the crew. She briefly addressed her outburst from the previous day, managing somewhat of an apology. Angie sent her with three insulated coffee pots and a variety of milk and sugar. She promised to check on the pots later, giving the woman her cell phone number in case of emergencies. Angie figured that Lucy hadn't meant her any harm. Maybe she was just really stressed out by her job.

The movie set turned out to be at one of the Island Harmony B&B cottages along the Sconset Bluff walk. The cottages had originally been a vacation colony back in the eighteen hundreds, and now were part of a B&B. The Sconset Bluff walk, a trail that cut through the back yards of some of the richest people on the island, went right past the cottages. There was even a wooden stairway that led down the bluff to the beach. As far as capturing the real "Nantucket Island" feel, about all they were missing was a widow's walk. The sides of the cottages were weathered gray shingles. The interiors were more modern, but with painted wood floors, big windows, and handmade quilts.

Now that the cat was out of the bag, as it were, rumors were pouring in. When Aunt Margery came in to work at ten, she had already collected some gossip.

The inside of one cottage had been redecorated to change one of the guest bedrooms to a den-slash-library. The film crew had brought all their own books, but apparently had brought all the *wrong* books for the character who owned the house, according to Aunt Margery's sources, the owners of the B&B. The kind of nurse who adopted strange men who had been hurt in a sailing accident did *not* read film history books, medical texts, and horror. That kind of nurse would read suspense and mystery, or, at least in Aunt Margery's opinion she would.

Most of the crew was staying at a tourist hotel in Nantucket. The stars and their assistants were staying at Jellicoe House, the same B&B that Walter had been staying in when his father had been murdered.

Jellicoe House was within easy walking distance of Nonatum's, the restaurant where she and Walter had broken up. The director, Al Petrillo, the writer, and a couple of gaffers were staying in another one of the Harmony B&B cottages so they could be close to the set. It was about eight miles from the bookstore to the cottages, not too far for a leisurely book delivery run via bicycle, but too far to ride for a coffee delivery first thing in the morning.

Back at the coffee shop, Sandra Potvin had overheard Aunt Margery talking about the books on the set and dragged someone over to meet her: the head writer, Hank Seaton. He was a man of average height with hair that was scruffed upward with gel into a tousled peak. The heels on his dress shoes were about an inch and a half high. He wore heavy black glasses and a silvery-gray suit with the tie loosened as if he had been hard at work all day. He instantly wrapped Aunt Margery around his finger by promising to look over what was on the shelves in the cottage and come over to the bookstore to rent titles to fill out the shelves correctly.

Hank and Aunt Margery were soon as thick as thieves, with Seaton quickly identifying Aunt Margery as a source for all things Nantucket, whether current, historical, rumored, or something that someone was trying to keep on the down-low. Within five minutes, he had extricated several pieces of gossip that almost made Angie choke on her coffee. Clearly, she had missed a *lot* of the who-was-sleeping-with-whom gossip lately. She loaded up her car with extra pots of coffee, a stack of books, and a couple of flyers for Sheldon's Shuckery. Sheldon was always helping her out; she might as well return the favor. Maybe she should take some cupcakes with her, too. She grabbed the first box she saw, a clean white box from The Nantucket Bakery.

As she was about to leave, she suddenly remembered that one of her older clients in Sconset had emailed last night, asking for some of the new mysteries that had come in a few days prior. Angie could do her book delivery at the same time as the coffee run. Mrs. Freeman would be delighted to get the books so early.

She walked over to the mystery shelves, grabbed the titles, then did a quick scan through the aisles to see if anyone needed anything.

Angie noticed that Ms. Potvin was leaning against a bookshelf with tears in her eyes, reading a heavy coffee-table book. Or rather she was staring at the book without really reading it. Her eyes didn't move as she stared at one of the open pages.

With a sniff, Ms. Potvin suddenly closed the book and slid it back on the shelf.

Angie delivered the coffee and the selection of the cupcakes she had pulled from the store, a dozen total. When she arrived, there was only about half a pot of coffee left; she made a mental note to bring four pots in the morning. The crew would be working straight through the rest of the weekend, apparently, although the stars would have the day off on Sunday.

Word was, on Monday the producer would be coming to the set. Whoever he was, he had left his mark. Low-grade anxiety seemed to swirl around like a bad smell. Stranger yet, when people saw the cupcakes that she had brought, they told her several times, independently, to bring a lot of cupcakes on Monday. They seemed almost scared to try any, everyone waving away her offer of a free cupcake. It was uncanny. Apparently, the producer had a real sweet tooth...and a bad temper whenever he had to restrain himself. It was considered bad luck to eat sweets on set because of him.

Angie was shown around the set. In the library, Al Petrillo asked her about the bookshelves. They hadn't filmed in the room yet, and he wanted to know if they really needed to redo the shelves, as Hank Seaton was insisting. Even though Al loved to read, he admitted, he really didn't have a sense of what anybody *else* liked to read, and the set designer had picked out the contents of the shelves herself. The set designer arrived on the scene and stated that she had chosen the types of books that the director had told her to pick out. Like some kind of comedy, the director then appeared. He was a younger man, named Joe Carbonneau, who looked like he could still be in college. He wore a Where's-Waldo-Style striped hat and stated that he wasn't a big reader, so he had asked for the types of books that he had seen on the producer's shelves.

Nobody was prepared to second-guess his taste in books without an expert opinion.

Angie said, "I'm sure my Aunt Margery, who is an even bigger book nerd than I am, would say that these shelves are completely wrong for your nurse character. But it's not like the viewers are going to be able to read the titles, right? I didn't see any directions for the characters to pick any of them up or read them, either. Does it even matter what books you use?"

That started another debate. Had she read the script? She had. In fact, she found that she had most of the characters' lines memorized. Did she have eidetic memory? No, she just really liked books. She read quickly and had a retentive memory for anything that interested her.

"But don't ask me what was in my math textbooks from high school," she said. They laughed.

The subject changed. Was the script, in her opinion, any good? They promised not to tell the writer her opinion, but she didn't believe them. "Ask Aunt Margery," she told them. "She's the writer in the family."

If Aunt Margery was the writer in the family, then what was Angie?

Her face turned beet red. "It's not important."

The set designer said, "I heard from the hotel desk clerk that I should check out the Pastries & Page-Turners bookstore downtown because the local detective owns it!"

Angie put a hand over her eyes. She wanted to curl up like a dead bug. "I'm not really a sleuth. I've just helped solve some murders, that's all."

As soon as she said it, she regretted it.

A sleuth! They all acted impressed and amused as she told them about the two murders that she had helped solve. "You must be named after Angela Lansbury," said the set designer, "from *Murder, She Wrote!*" And then Angie had to explain that no, her real name was Agatha Mary Clarissa Christie Prouty and she'd been named after the Queen of Crime. She eyeballed the door of the library, beginning to plan her escape, thinking she could point at a book on the far side of the room and make a break for it while they were all looking the other way. Her face was burning hot with embarrassment.

"But I'm not really a sleuth," she kept insisting. That was just what her family called her. Well, everyone on the set would start calling her that, too, just give it a few days! Angie wanted to die.

Fortunately, they all had better things to do than make fun of her all morning. Al had to shoot some exterior shots of the cottage and the beach. He called someone on his cell phone, then told the director, "Your great-aunt says she'll be right over. Hank's bringing her over in his car." It was agreed: Aunt Margery would be brought onto the set as their book consultant. A ridiculous amount of money, not quite a month's rent for the store, but more than they were paying to rent her books, was mentioned as a consultancy fee. The viewers might not notice the books on the set, but the actors would. Julia Withers was famous for subconsciously adjusting her character to fit with the setting—even when that adjustment wasn't appropriate.

"What if the producer isn't happy with the book selection?" Angie asked.

The others looked grimly at each other.

"Maybe he won't notice," Angie said.

"He'll notice," the director muttered. They all looked depressed.

Angie said, "At least he won't be able to steamroll Aunt Margery out of her opinion." They didn't believe her. "Just wait," she said, realizing that none of them had met Aunt Margery yet. "She has *very* strong opinions about books."

"The producer's name is Lance Mitchell," Aunt Margery announced triumphantly upon her return from the movie set, where she had spent most of the day being buttered up by Hank, the writer. Angie was frantically trying to get next week's book orders in before Janet left for the day, so she wasn't in the best mood when her great-aunt interrupted her. A new book had come out, *Delusions of Filmmaking: A Novel of a Dirty Rotten Hollywood Scoundrel,* an anonymous, fictionalized tell-all on the film industry, and she only had three copies on her shelves. Considering that the island was full of film people at the moment, she probably needed a couple dozen.

"Oh?"

"And he had an affair with the lead actress, Julia Withers."

That set Angie back for a moment. Julia didn't strike her as the kind of person who would sleep around to get ahead in her career, and the producer sounded like a real piece of work. A minor mystery.

"She was here for a while yesterday," Angie said. "I think she's trying to keep a low profile, though, so she's avoiding us today, so the tourists don't turn the store into a circus."

"What is she like?"

"She seems too adorable to be true, but really she's just too adorable. And Captain Parfait likes her." She told the story about the cat.

Aunt Margery snorted, but said, "If Captain Parfait likes her, that's good enough for me. Anyways, we need to start pulling books from the shelves. I have quite the list. Oh! And while I was there, guess who should appear?"

"Santa and his eight tiny reindeer?"

"Very funny. It was Sheldon! He brought samples of lobster rolls to the set, to persuade everyone to avoid the Nonatum and to change their allegiance to the Shuckery by bribery!"

"Um, I think it just counts as good marketing," Angie said, feeling a little self-conscious about bringing a box full of cupcakes.

"Bribery!" Aunt Margery chortled. "Mind you, I can't blame him. Now, let's get to sorting out these books."

And then she produced an *enormous* list, sheets and sheets of legal-pad paper.

Angie sighed. More work. It would mean another chunk of profit, though, and they would totally be able to brag about the fact that their books had been featured on the set of a movie, even if it was just a TV movie. She should send Janet to the set to take some pictures after the books had been set up.

The rest of the day was busy, but not crazy-busy. Janet left. She promised to handle the deliveries in the morning, then check up on the set again around ten a.m. with her camera to get some photos. The number of books that they wanted on the set was enough to deplete a lot of the shelves. Fortunately, a bunch of crew members arrived to load the books into the Microbuses and haul them to the set themselves, so Angie didn't have to do it. They even took Aunt Margery with them to advise them on how to organize the books.

Angie was left to restock the shelves as best she could with the stock she had on hand. She made strategic use of bookends, knickknacks, and other small items for sale to fill out the shelves. The three copies of the tell-all book, *Delusions of Filmmaking*, were moved to her new releases rack in the front of the store along with several other film books. There were tourists inside the store, but fortunately they weren't the kind of tourists who got stuffy about having to step around boxes of rearranged books. They were all impressed by the fact that the books were going to a "star" on a movie set. They also all wanted to know where the set was so they could visit.

Angie totally threw the movie crew under the bus and told the tourists where they were filming. It wasn't like the news hadn't gotten out already. She might have lost a little business by sending her customers away, but at least she got the peace of mind of having a nearly empty store as she rearranged her shelves.

As she worked, she remembered the book that Ms. Potvin had been reading. Angie had already pulled it off the shelves with the rest of the film books, but she hadn't really looked at it.

It was an oversized coffee table book called *Nouvelle Vague: How the French Broke Free of Psychological Realism with New Wave Cinema, 1958–1969*. It was by none other than Lance Mitchell, and it had been published in 2003. Angie's copy was a first edition, unsigned but in near-fine condition, just a few scuffs on the dust jacket.

She set it aside to read later. She wasn't expecting much. The man sounded arrogant, and people like him rarely wrote good books.

But she didn't want it sitting around to upset the rest of the crew. Apparently, they were going to have enough to deal with on Monday morning when he arrived.

## Chapter 4

# MONSIEUR NOUVELLE VAGUE

When Angie arrived at the store on Sunday morning, she had completely changed her opinion. Lance Mitchell wasn't just a good writer, he was a great one. He had taken the subject of New Wave Cinema, which she had known nothing about, and turned it into a subject that she felt that she understood enough to be able to discuss intelligently with just about anybody. His passion for the subject was obvious. His sensitivity in explaining it, however, was something she hadn't even remotely expected.

Besides reading the book, she had watched parts of several of the most important movies he had listed in the book. She didn't have time to do more than that. The movies seemed jerky and almost unprofessional, but that made her feel that the amateurish techniques were used in a purposeful way. Weird cuts, shaky cameras...it all seemed very sophisticated somehow.

She didn't think that she would be able to keep up an entire conversation with anyone on the film crew about the book, at least not until she had watched the rest of the movies that she had bought and downloaded the previous night. She had a better appreciation of the man himself, though he seemed like one of the French *auteurs* he wrote about, very demanding but all for the sake of his vision.

She wondered if he would stop by the bookstore while he was on Nantucket. She hoped so.

The entire crew seemed slightly depressed that morning, or at least a little repressed. They were quieter. Some of the people who had been in the store on both Friday and Saturday hadn't even bothered to show up.

What was wrong with everyone?

The bell on the door rang. It was about nine a.m., after the worst of the rush, and Angie was straightening up the café area, wiping tables, refolding the newspapers, straightening pillows, emptying trash cans, and checking on customers.

When she looked up, a handsome man in a suit was standing in the doorway, looking around and straightening his French cuffs. He had salt-and-pepper hair, and was the epitome of the word "distinguished."

She immediately knew who he was. He looked just like he had in his author photo. Almost. Where he had been a tousled man of thirty-five in the photo, which had been taken on a boat with the wind in his hair, here he was a polished, but still handsome older professional.

Wasn't he supposed to arrive on Monday, not Sunday?

Regardless, arrived he had.

"So, this is where you've been hiding," he said sardonically to the lingering crew members in the café area of the bookstore. "No, please don't get up. I'm sure you're just taking a well-earned break."

Nobody laughed, nobody smiled.

Suddenly, Angie didn't want to compliment this jerk on his book. Apparently, he'd changed a lot since he'd written it.

He strode up to the counter, his burgundy-wine-colored shoes impeccably polished.

He turned his gaze to Angie and ordered with just one word.

"Espresso."

Trying to keep calm and not show any of her emotions on her face, she started pulling a shot.

He was sneering at her almost before she began.

"This is why I hate leaving LA." He said as he pinched the bridge of his nose and gritted his teeth.

He stepped around the counter and motioned with one hand for Angie to step out of the way.

He proceeded to dump out the ground coffee she had loaded into the puck, reload it himself, and pull a shot of espresso. "When was the last time you calibrated this? Never mind, don't answer that. I'm sure it was when you bought it. Do you even know how to calibrate it? It's a crap machine anyway. You should have a La Pavoni. And don't pull into an espresso mug. What are you doing, eyeballing your pulls? That's an amateur hour move. Get a Pyrex beaker with shot measurements on the side."

He waved a hand toward her bean grinder. "And you're buying your beans pre-roasted, which is typical small-town coffee crap. God, I miss LA. You need to get a roaster and start roasting your own. I don't care if there's no roaster on the island. Get a decent tabletop model for under five grand. You cannot get good coffee out of rancid beans."

He pulled the shot while looking at his Rolex. Crema rose to the top of the shot, covering it with caramel-colored foam. "At least you don't have ten thousand sugar syrups to try to cover up the taste. But try, would you, to get some decent chocolate syrup for your mochas? The stuff you have here is garbage."

The member of the film crew who was nearest the counter happened to be Sandra Potvin. With her eyes narrowed, she said, "You should try the cupcakes, Lance. Not even *you* could criticize them."

Lance shot Sandra a look dirty enough to make Angie's skin crawl. She was surprised by the obvious animosity between the two. The whole crew seemed pretty transparent about how Lance made them feel.

Someone, Angie didn't see whom, called out, "Yeah, Mister Low Blood Sugar, try the cupcake!"

Lance Mitchell glared at the room and bent down, looking inside the pastry case. He quickly grabbed one of the mincemeat cupcakes, taking a big bite off the top. "I hear you're the one who brought the cupcakes to the set yesterday. I'll have whatever cupcakes you have left. Unlike the coffee, those were made with care. The one I had on set this morning was pretty good."

Angie dug under the counter and found an old brown box buried underneath some boxes of utensils. She placed the remainder of the cupcakes inside it.

Lance handed her the perfect little demitasse of espresso, putting the cup on a saucer and placing it on the counter in front of her. "I don't have time to hang around and do your job for you, but hopefully you have learned something today." He stepped away from her, looked her up and down as if assessing her entire image, and said, "Taste that. You could be making espresso *at least* that good, even if you never took another step toward improving the quality of your supplies and equipment."

He looked around the room, spotted the rack of new releases toward the front, and sneered at a copy of the book *Delusions of Filmmaking*. He picked up the book and displayed it to the staff. "You all know this book is about me, even if the names are changed. It's a book full of lies and I'm going to sue the author for everything they are worth and more. My lawyers are terrific." He strode toward the exit and dropped the other half of the mincemeat cupcake in the trash before slamming the door behind him.

Angie blinked slowly, trying to process what had just happened. She was still holding the espresso.

She sipped it. Okay, he wasn't wrong. She could be doing better on the café side of her business. Her real love was the books, though. But he'd barely even looked at them. His shot of espresso was better than the ones she was making, and she felt like it was a matter of pride to improve hers until they were better than *his*. That would show him.

She put the cup and saucer down on the counter. She needed to think of the perfect thing to say to defuse the situation. Something witty and cutting.

"Wooooowwww," she said. "*And* he forgot his cupcakes," Angie swept her hands over to the brown cupcake box that remained on the countertop.

Smiles cracked across the somber faces in the room. The people in the film crew started laughing uproariously. The few tourists in the store almost seemed to melt with relief. What she had said hadn't been that funny, but it had been a tense situation.

Janet, who had been working in the back, stuck out her head. "Is it safe to come out?"

More laughter. Angie drank the rest of the espresso thoughtfully, leaning back against the counter over the fridge. If only Aunt Margery had been there. She would have cut him down with some well-worded literary quote that would have burned him down to his soul.

She wanted to be there when the two of them first met. With popcorn.

Wow. Just wow.

## Chapter 5

## DIRTY ROTTEN HOLLYWOOD SCOUNDREL

That night Angie called Jo, whom she hadn't seen or talked to since the kayaking expedition. She completely forgot about wanting to tease her and pretend to be angry. She had been so busy that she forgot that she was even annoyed in the first place.

"Are you okay?" Jo asked, sounding slightly worried.

"No! Do you know what happened to me today?"

"What? You're not still mad at me, right?"

Angie quickly reassured her that all was fine. She sometimes forgot how worried Jo could get if she thought Angie was mad at her.

"But listen!" Angie said afterward. "You should have *seen* this guy. The producer."

"Lance Mitchell," Jo said in a hard voice. "Oh, I've seen him. He stopped by the bakery to buy a box of cupcakes."

"Oh, no. Are you okay?"

Jo said, "*I'm* fine."

Angie felt the hairs on the back of her neck stand up. "Is Mickey okay?"

"He's gone quiet. Not the good kind of quiet, either."

It had been a long time since Angie had seen Mickey go quiet, but it was something to remember. In middle school, Mickey, who was normally the class clown, had gone for six months without talking. At all. No matter how much detention or session time with the school counselor he was given, he wouldn't speak. A bully had been picking on a girl; Mickey had stood up for her; the principal had believed the bully's story and completely ignored the story of Mickey and the girl. The bully had been the daughter of one of the wealthier families on the island.

The other girl had been Angie.

"What did Mitchell *do*?" Angie asked.

"He said something about you," Jo said. "It wasn't nice. I just about killed him. You can imagine how Mickey took it."

Angie sighed. Mickey was one of her best friends. They had dated in high school briefly, and, during her last sleuthing gig, they had a few moments where those old feelings started to emerge. "So, you heard about it already. I don't need to tell you."

"Oh, you can tell me. In great length. While I'm planning to kill him."

"Do I need to come over?"

"Yes, please. I'll tell Mickey that you're upset, and you need his support. And some wine. That should make him come over. And then you can try to get him to talk."

Angie arrived at Jo's apartment. Jo wanted to make sure that Angie was still okay with going to the punk show and hadn't changed her mind. "I'm really going to order you some steel-toed books, I mean boots," she said.

Angie laughed. "Uh-huh. I'm going to wish I'd gone to the movie instead."

"We could do both. The first night, we'll go to the remake of *Mutiny* starring Rob Blake and some chick who can't hold a candle to Angela Lansbury, and the punk show the next."

"Wouldn't it be better to do it the other way around?"

"*Mutiny* is a swashbuckling movie that will make your blood boil. I want you showing your rage at this punk show. Avast, ye punk!"

Angie laughed. They'd known each other forever. Jo knew how to cheer her up.

When Mickey showed up, he had two bottles of wine in each hand, held by the necks. He slammed all four down on Jo's beat-up, stained, paper-and-game-controller-covered coffee table. From the look on his face, she wouldn't have been surprised if his eyes had flickered with tiny fires.

"You okay?" Angie said.

He swallowed. "Red wine for a blood feud," he said, his voice croaking.

"Open the first bottle. We should let it breathe."

Mickey opened the wine and poured it into Jo's wine carafe. Jo was completely non-fancy in most ways, but absurdly fussy in others. If she was gonna drink wine, it was gonna be properly aerated when she drank it.

"So, you had an encounter with Lance Mitchell," Angie said. It was better not to beat around the bush where Mickey was concerned.

Mickey took a deep breath. "He said you were an incompetent barista. That you were a joke. And that your book selection left much to be desired. He thought the only reason you were still open was that our bakery was supporting you."

"He said something similar while he was in the bookstore," Angie said. "With almost the entire film crew, a few tourists, and about a dozen regulars in the store."

Mickey put a hand over his face.

"It's okay. I laughed it off," Angie said.

"What?!"

"Well, he wasn't wrong," she said. "I *am not* a natural barista, and the beans we use *are* kind of inferior because they're not fresh-roasted. *And* I need to take care of my equipment and put some consistent rules in place. But most of my book selection was, hint, hint, on his shelves on the movie set, so there wasn't much left in the store. And he's not a small businessman who runs a retail space. He probably has no idea how much multitasking I have to do."

"But none of those things are funny," Mickey said. "How can you laugh about it?"

"Says the class clown," Angie said, throwing the wine cork over to him. "I think what really set him off was this book he saw. A book called..." She went to her handbag and pulled out a copy, setting it on the table in front of him. *"Delusions of Filmmaking: A Novel of a Dirty Rotten Hollywood Scoundrel.* By that great author, Anonymous."

Mickey frowned at the book. "What's it about?"

"It's a thinly-veiled account of a naïve film-school student becoming a famous, and infamously unethical Hollywood producer, only to find that he's not as unethical as the top-tier Hollywood producers. It sounds almost exactly like Lance Mitchell's Wikipedia page but with the names changed."

Jo said, "Do you think he wrote it himself?"

"Nope. He said he was planning to sue the author."

"I'll buy a copy," Jo said. "I'll buy two copies and sneak one onto the film set."

Angie almost choked on her Zinfandel. "No. Just...no."

Mickey asked, "What's so bad about it?"

"I only glanced at a few pages. But yes, okay, one of the first things we find out is that the main character, Mike France aka Lance Mitchell, took credit for the work of other people. Basically, it says he wrote a famous book on French cinema, but that someone else actually wrote most of it."

Mickey whistled softly. "Didn't Lance Mitchell write a book on French cinema? Uh..." he made a circular gesture with one hand as he struggled to remember the title.

"*Nouvelle Vague* is the name of the book that Lance Mitchell supposedly wrote by himself, yes. So, this new book, *Delusions of Filmmaking*, accuses him of taking sole credit for the *Nouvelle Vague* book and ignoring some mysterious co-author."

"That's quite an accusation for one to make. Maybe he could sue the publisher or something, since the book was published anonymously."

She chewed on her lip. "The author would have had to sign something in her contract with the publisher indemnifying the publisher against any charges of libel. Mitchell *could* sue, I suppose, and the publisher might be forced to give up the name of the author. But that he would identify himself with the character kind of implies that he did steal the book credit, and maybe the royalties as well. I think that any suit against the co-writer might bring out *a lot* of dirty laundry."

"Do you think the author of this book is lying or telling the truth?"

Angie shook her head. "It's not going to matter. It's going to damage Lance Mitchell's reputation either way. This book is a juicy little bit of evil Hollywood fluff. It's wicked and cynical and dark and fun to read. If the rest of the book is as good, it's going to be a bestseller."

## Chapter 6

# EVERYONE'S FAVORITE DAY
# OF THE WEEK

At two a.m., Angie went home for the night, walking because she was too drunk to drive and too sober to trust Jo's alarm clock to wake her up.

At four-thirty a.m., Angie was jolted awake from a nightmare she couldn't remember. It was close enough to her normal waking hour that she decided to get up and make herself some coffee. She was still a little drunk. She walked out to Brant Point, feeling the bite of a storm in the air. It was still possible that they could get some snow in April, even if most of it would melt as it hit the ground. She caught moisture on her skin in tiny prickles that could have been snow or rain, or tiny bits of half-frozen slush. The tide was annoyed at having to encounter an island first thing in the morning, and sloshed grumpily against the sand, throwing up sea foam and smashing shells.

She picked up a piece of dark blue sea glass and put it in her pocket.

Angie went in to work at six a.m. With expanded staffing had come expanded hours, and she had called in favors from Janet one too many times that week. *Someone* had to run the store on a cold, wet Monday morning, everyone's favorite day of the week. Guess who? But they were planning to close the store on Tuesday, so at least tomorrow would be a day off.

The store was quiet and peaceful, and Captain Parfait was in a friendly mood. She was able to get a lot of work done before six-thirty, when she flipped over the sign in the front door and let in her regulars.

None of the film crew came. Honestly, she wasn't expecting them to. After the incident with Lance, she assumed they wouldn't be returning. Ever again.

Her regulars made a point of loudly complimenting her coffee, the pastries, the book selection, even the carpet. They were sweethearts. Mickey brought over pastries right after she opened. It was pretty clear from the look on his face that he hadn't gotten any sleep.

"What do you think about Nantucket Bakery and Coffee Roasters?" he said. "We already have a great distribution system set up."

"Lot of investment capital."

"Jo says she's going to blackmail a certain film producer for the cash to buy the roaster and our first batch of beans, as well as advertising material."

"She's a very thorough blackmailer. Tell her I approve."

He left.

By seven a.m. she decided that if any of the film crew was ever going to come back, at least some of them would have come by then.

Jo called a few minutes later. "Angie," she whispered over the phone.

"What is it?" Angie whispered back.

"Lance Mitchell is—" Angie didn't quite make out the word.

"What?"

Jo repeated herself. It was still garbled.

"He's there?" Angie said. "At the store?"

"Not at the store!" Jo hissed. "And keep your voice down. The cops are here."

The cold hand of fear clasped itself around Angie's heart.

"Why are the cops there?"

"Because they think we did it," Jo said. "I'm not clear on the details yet. Detective Bailey and the others just got here. They're questioning Mickey right now. They're going to question me in a minute. He's dead, Angie. Lance is dead!"

"He's dead," Angie repeated, goosebumps rising on her arms. "Lance Mitchell is dead."

"Didn't I just say that?"

"What was it? How did he die?"

Jo lowered her voice even further and said something. Angie blinked. Had she heard her right?

"Did you just say he was *poisoned*?"

"They think it might have been in the cupcakes," Jo whispered. Her voice was tight. "He ate almost every single one of the cupcakes that you brought to the set on Saturday *and* the ones we sold him on Sunday."

Angie shook her head, more than a little incredulous. "Should I come over?"

"No! They're coming over to your place next. Get ready, that's all I'm saying." She hung up.

Angie looked around the store. If she called Janet to come in and cover the store while she was being questioned, then the police would know that Jo or Mickey had called her. She was a hundred percent sure that Jo wasn't supposed to have called her to warn her, and also a hundred percent sure that Detective Bailey would be angry if he found out.

Anyone on the set could have known about Lance Mitchell's sweet tooth, but not everyone could have put poison into one of the cupcakes.

It was essential to find out what kind of poison was in the cupcakes.

Detective Bailey would be there soon.

Detective Bailey was the detective for Nantucket Island. Being the only detective on a small island, he didn't have too many murders or other serious crimes to investigate, especially in the off-season. In fact, he spent most of his time working on petty theft cases or tourist traffic accidents. He was a born Nantucket local just like Angie, but he was a few years older than she was, and they hadn't spent a lot of time around each other.

At least, that is, they hadn't spent a lot of time around each other until she had started solving crimes. Detective Bailey had reluctantly joined forces with Angie for the two murders that had taken place on the island. With the assistance of a local, he could make surprising advancements on cases. Angie's natural curiosity and genetic nosiness, paired with Bailey's frequent need to get a second set of eyes on his work, made the two an unlikely but successful pair.

Angie had started out thinking that Detective Bailey disliked her personally, but she was starting to suspect he just didn't like the idea of having a civilian nosing around in evidence that he was going to get blamed for screwing up. He was tall, single, and fairly handsome, but also too intimidating, blunt, and humorless to find attractive. He had always been rather unapproachable. Angie had faint memories of him from elementary school, standing aside seriously at the sandbox while the other kids played.

Detective Bailey entered Pastries & Page-Turners through the back door, only announcing himself by softly clearing his throat. Angie was on her own, serving customers. Aunt Margery wouldn't be in until at least ten a.m.

"I'm sorry, Detective Bailey, I don't have anyone to cover for me at the moment," she said when he asked if she could step into the back for a few moments. "Can this wait until I can call Aunt Margery and have her come in?"

Detective Bailey chewed his lip for a moment, then lifted a finger in a *one moment* gesture and called the police station on his cell phone, asking for backup at Pastries & Page-Turners. After a moment of negotiation over who would be sent, he hung up.

"I'm afraid it can't wait as long as it would take to get your great-aunt out of bed early, Miss Angie. I don't know if a saint could wait that long, and I'm working on an investigation, so I'm even less patient than normal. I'll have one of the deputies watch the store while we talk."

"Thank you."

She wasn't sure whether it was a good idea or not, but at least the short delay gave her time to get caught up on her regulars, who all wanted to know where the film crew was and why Detective Bailey had come to the store.

Angie told them the crew was probably just on an early outdoor shoot and she wasn't sure what Detective Bailey wanted. Outside, the sky was overcast with heavy clouds, which would probably make the outdoor shots too dark, but none of the regulars seemed to catch her in the fib.

The deputy came in and was quickly instructed on what to do. He was a young man who had previously worked at one of the big coffee chains, thank goodness, and only needed a bit of instruction on how to run the cash register. She gave Detective Bailey the nod. He had been sitting among her regulars, reading a copy of *Time* magazine. He set it aside and followed her into the back room.

They could both hear the regulars speculating about what had happened. They moved as far as they could from the front of the store, back to the thrift-store armchair where Angie retreated on her breaks to read a book. She offered him the chair, but he shook his head and leaned against the wall next to a poster of Stephen King promoting libraries.

"I'm sure you've heard," he said.

She wanted to pretend that she hadn't, but it was useless. The truth would come out. "About Lance Mitchell being dead? Only very briefly. I don't know the details."

He nodded but didn't answer the implied question. "I understand that you had a confrontation with the man yesterday."

"I did. He came into the store and explained to me in no uncertain terms that my coffee was terrible." She felt her hands tense on the arms of the chair, not out of fear that Detective Bailey would get it in his head that she had attacked the man, but because she was still hurt and upset about the episode. That he hadn't exactly been wrong was the worst part of it, too.

"I also understand, until yesterday's confrontation at least, that your store had become a gathering-place for many on the film crew."

"It had."

"Because you called in a favor from Miss Jerritt after she took you out onto the Sound to watch the shooting of a scene near Whale Rock, and you urged them to come to the bookstore for coffee afterwards."

"Yes."

This was sounding worse and worse, as if she had a serious grudge against Lance Mitchell.

"Would you say that the arrival of Mr. Mitchell caused a significant loss to your business?"

"I would say that it cut off the windfall of the extra business that they brought to the store, but not actually a loss."

"Is it true that Julia Withers came to your store?"

"Yes, she did. But only once. She was worried that word of her presence would get out, and that she would be mobbed by fans."

"You didn't tell anyone that she was here?"

"I wouldn't say that. I told several people. Aunt Margery, Jo, Mickey, and..." She frowned. Had she told Carol? "Maybe Carol Brightwell. I can't remember."

"You didn't announce it publicly in any way, for example, on social media?"

She frowned. They could just check that, couldn't they? "No. And I don't think Janet or Aunt Margery did, either. We've had a number of famous people here before. We don't make it a habit of announcing their presence, and I've talked to Janet about how to handle it if she does encounter someone like that."

"You didn't announce anything else about the production to your customers?"

"I did tell a bunch of them that they were filming at Island Harmony B&B. I wanted to encourage them to leave the store at the moment... I'm not proud of it, but I was tired and feeling more than a little overwhelmed."

"Overwhelmed by what?"

"Aunt Margery convinced the writer and several other key members on the set that they needed to replace the books on set because they were out of character. She talked them into renting about a third of the books in the store, which I had to pull off the shelves and box up, then put out more stock and rearrange things so the shelves didn't look so bare. My back hurt and I was short-tempered at the time."

He nodded again. "Can you describe your experience, overall, with the members of the crew?"

She closed her eyes and leaned her head back for a moment. "They were polite."

"In more detail, please?"

She told him everything she could remember; this took some time. He stopped her after a few moments to take out a notebook. He jotted down some notes, then gestured at her to continue. By the time she had finished, she felt like she had described the plot of a fairly intricate novel.

"Thank you. And now please describe your confrontation with Mr. Mitchell."

She took a deep breath, trying to keep from reacting emotionally. She didn't want to get emotional over something so essentially unimportant. The scene with Mitchell took less time to describe. After all, it had only taken a few minutes to tear her day in half, before and after.

"And can you sum up the rest of the day, both at the store and afterwards?"

She was already tired of answering questions and this wasn't even the official statement. She wished she was reading a book, so she could skim ahead. Detective Bailey stopped her several times to ask her when everyone had been in the store, when they had left, who else had come in, when *they* had left, and so on. Then she described spending the evening with the Jerritt twins.

"And did any of you leave, once you had arrived at Miss Jerritt's apartment?"

"I walked home at two a.m. I was too drunk to drive. So did Mickey. He walked, I mean."

"Did he go to his apartment?"

"I presume so? We had to go in different directions."

Something in the back of her head was trying to get her attention.

"And what did you do this morning?"

Another description. He stopped her suddenly at the point where she described having forgotten to take the trash out the night before and had to put the bags out this morning.

"Can you point out the trash bag for the can at the front door?"

It was like being poked in the side. "That was it! He threw half the cupcake away."

"Yes, ma'am, and I'd like to get it."

"Do you think it was poisoned? It couldn't possibly have been directed toward him, if so."

"I'm not at liberty to speculate, Miss Angie."

"I think I can find it." She led him to the trash bins behind the store. They weren't as filthy as some she'd seen in Boston, which was the best that could be said about them. She had two types of trash bags for the store, big gray bags for the café garbage at the counter, and small black bags for the trash cans scattered throughout the store. The recyclables went into a separate, bagless bin.

Which one, though, she had no idea.

"It's in one of the smaller bags," she said.

If Detective Bailey wanted her to dig through the bags to find a specific half-eaten cupcake, the answer was no. But instead, he thanked her and sent her inside to relieve the deputy from his duty as temporary barista. The deputy gave her a pitiable look when she warned him about what was in store for him. She found him a pair of disposable gloves and showed him what kind of cupcake he was looking for: brown gingerbread cake with a white cream cheese frosting and a center oozing with apples and raisins.

After a night in a trash bag, it was sure to be especially appealing.

After a few moments, Detective Bailey reappeared. She finished with her customer. The deputy had done well enough with the coffee and cash register. Most of the regulars had come up to the counter to tell her so.

Angie looked at Detective Bailey. "Yes, detective?" None of her customers were too near the counter at the moment. "Am I under arrest for the possible murder of an extremely rude movie producer?"

"No, ma'am," Detective Bailey said, with a completely straight face. "It seems that you wouldn't benefit much from his death, didn't have much of a motive, and had a decent alibi for the time in question."

"When was the time in question? Last night with Jo and Mickey?"

He shook his head once. "This morning."

"This *morning*? When did he die? I wouldn't have thought he'd even be awake yet this morning."

"I can't go into any details, ma'am."

"I'll just ask Jo and Mickey," she pointed out.

He grimaced.

"What, did you arrest them?"

"Not yet." He left via the back door even before she could wipe the shocked expression off her face.

## Chapter 7

## NEVER LOVE AGAIN

Carol Brightwell stopped by the bookstore just after Aunt Margery arrived and took up position at the large desk next to the coffee counter. Aunt Margery was, as the saying went, getting up there in years, and rightfully refused to stand on her feet all day. Angie had set up a second credit card machine and a computer at the desk so that Aunt Margery could work on inventory, ordering, and bookkeeping tasks without having to get up and use the system in the back room.

She suspected her great-aunt of writing a sensational novel about sex, backstabbing, and millionaires on Nantucket when she, Angie, wasn't looking.

As long as the inventory got done and the receipts were all entered, though, Angie didn't mind. The main benefit of having Aunt Margery come in at midmorning was that Angie didn't have to try to get her up any earlier in the day. Other benefits included having all of Aunt Margery's friends, gossips each one of them, come into the store throughout the latter part of the day for coffee. It was an island network of as much juicy gossip as anyone could wish for. It was also a kind of informal small business association meeting, since a lot of Aunt Margery's friends also owned shops around the island.

Carol wasn't one of Aunt Margery's close friends; she was too optimistic and cheerful for that, and she was from the Hudson Valley area—*very* exclusive. "I'm *so* relieved you're on the case!" she exclaimed as she entered the store from the back door.

Angie glanced up. She was tackling the boxes of books the mail had brought earlier, putting together the orders that needed to be hand-delivered around the island.

"I'm on the case?" she said.

"Yes, and I'm so relieved," Carol said firmly.

Angie suddenly realized that Carol was expecting her to dig into the murder like she had done twice before. "Carol, I hate to tell you, but that's not really me. I have a store to run."

The last murder Angie had solved was when her dear friend was murdered during a treasure hunt on the island. Carol had been very grateful to have that murder solved; unsolved murders were bad business for the island, and for the chamber.

"So, you aren't looking into it?" said Carol with a furrowed brow.

"This is too big for me. A big-time movie producer from Hollywood? And a Hollywood film crew? This isn't a bunch of tourists or us locals anymore. I'm a bookseller and café owner. And, in case you haven't heard, I was brutally reminded that I'm not even that great at it."

"You do know that the Jerritt twins, your friends, are suspects on the case."

"Nobody can seriously think that. They had no reason to want the man dead. He was a big fan of their cupcakes."

"But you're still going to look into it, right?"

Angie put down the box cutter she was holding. Her hand was gripping it just a little too tightly. "As I just said, Carol, I can't."

"I think it would be best if you at least spent a little time on it. These murders are not good for the local businesses. The island needs a sleuth."

"The island has Detective Bailey," Angie said firmly. "And whatever other officers that are sent from Boston to assist him in this matter. I'm sure he won't have to handle all this on his own."

Carol digested what Angie said, and then opened her eyes brightly as if she had just come up with a brilliant idea. "I'll have a word with your Aunt Margery about it."

"I'm sure several people have had words about it with her already."

Carol Brightwell left a few minutes later, looking a little forced in her good cheer. Angie gave her a wave. She didn't like to say no to the woman, but her assumption had been ridiculous. Angie wasn't a detective. She had no training. She had other things to do.

Angie felt like she had lead weights in her stomach. The last time someone had died, it had been a friend of hers – Reed Edgerton – and she had almost thought that she had lost Mickey, too. What next? *Who* next? If she had been spending time standing next to another murderer, she didn't want to know. She didn't want to have any more nightmares about that person standing next to her in line at the grocery store, giving her a smile, and threatening to kill her great-aunt if she talked to the police. She'd had enough of them already.

She wasn't Aunt Margery, who loved dark and juicy gossip more than she loved sugar in her coffee. She wasn't Detective Bailey, either, who was getting paid to see the world the way a cop has to see it.

Part of her just wanted to solve murders like they were logic puzzles. A clever challenge where nobody really died, and you just filled in a bunch of checkboxes lining up motive, method, and opportunity.

That her first case had been investigating the murder of Walter's father didn't help. She had thought she was okay with breaking up with Walter, but all morning she had been thinking about him and his father's murder all over again.

"I have to get out of here," she muttered. Fortunately, she was able to quickly put together her deliveries and load them into the basket of her bicycle.

Al Petrillo needed more books. He'd emailed her to say that he would understand if Pastries & Page-Turners didn't want to do any further business with the production, but that he would be forced to start rereading books if she didn't. He didn't dare touch the shelves, and shelves, and shelves of books that Aunt Margery had brought over to the library set. They were filming in there, and "as sure as God made little green apples," he said, "*someone* would spot a difference if he removed, or even moved, a single book on the shelves."

He didn't have to say who that *someone* was. Angie understood.

It was a cry for help, or at least a cry for peace. She picked through some of the newer titles that had come in that morning and wrapped up another package for him.

"I'll be back later," she called to Aunt Margery, and then left before she could be called over to hear the latest gossip.

But Aunt Margery was wilier than she had anticipated. As Angie was bicycling on the trail alongside Milestone Road, a car pulled up alongside her, an old Toyota land cruiser that she immediately recognized as belonging to Dory Jerritt. Mickey and Jo's mother.

She had been involved in one of Angie's previous murder cases.

Intimately.

The window rolled down, and Dory waved at Angie. With a sigh, Angie rolled to a stop. Dory got out and walked over to her. She was a fireplug of a woman, with broad shoulders, a jaw that always seemed to jut out stubbornly, and an attitude to match.

"Hello, Angie. Do you have a moment?"

Better to get this over with.

"Of course."

"Word is that my children are suspected of murdering someone, and that you don't intend to do anything about it."

Trying to control her temper in the face of the woman's blunt attitude, Angie said, "Jo and Mickey aren't actually suspected of murdering anyone, as far as I know."

"Don't try to double-talk me," Dory said. "You know how this works. Their cupcakes were involved. They're suspects. So nobody actually told you they were suspects, so what? You're supposed to do something about it."

Dory had lied during the previous case, lied in such a way that Angie had never gotten over it and had never really forgiven her. She felt a sticky, hot sensation in her chest, the worst sort of petty anger. Angie looked the woman right in the eyes. She had never been the queen of staring contests, but she didn't seem to be having any trouble at the moment. "Say that again."

Stubbornly, Dory said, "You're supposed to do something about it."

About a hundred different responses flashed through Angie's mind. She finally just shook her head and started bicycling forward. She was about to say something unforgivable, she knew it. Dory walked alongside the bicycle.

"You're supposed to do something about it!" Dory shouted at her.

Angie pedaled faster. *She doesn't deserve a response. I refuse to get in a shouting match with her right now. Jo would spit if she were here right now. Dory is one of Aunt Margery's best friends. I have to keep my cool.*

Dory Jerritt didn't have the right to demand anything of her. She didn't even buy her books from Angie's bookstore.

She followed Angie for a dozen feet, then stopped.

"You're supposed to do something about it!"

By the time that Angie had made it to Island Harmony B&B, she had managed to cool down. Stopping to talk to her customers and deliver their books helped. She didn't tell anyone about Lance Mitchell being dead. Instead, she had talked briefly to each person about her favorite subject: books. It felt like taking a mini-vacation with her toes in the sand. Really, it did.

They weren't filming at Island Harmony B&B that day, which was just as well. Although one of the extras had arrived at the bookstore earlier, begging for coffee anyway. She had completely forgotten— the interview with Detective Bailey had driven it out of her mind. She had mostly just assumed that everyone would be too terrified of Lance Mitchell to have anything more to do with the bookstore, although of course his death changed the situation somewhat. But apparently it had been a case of "the show must go on," and they planned to resume filming in the next day or two, and if nothing else, they all wanted to show their support of her coffee-making skills.

She still felt awkward pulling up beside the main building at the cottages. She walked up to the front door, and some sort of assistant with a badge greeted her.

She said, "Hello, my name is Angie Prouty, and I'm looking for Al Petrillo. I have his books."

"His books? Didn't he just get a bunch of boxes full of books?"

"He did. This is a personal order, from the same store."

The assistant pulled out a cell phone. "He's in the smaller of the two cottages. Just go up to the door and ask for him there."

"Thanks."

She left the bike against the side of the building and walked along a pretty brick path to the cottages. A short white picket fence separated the main yard from the cottage area. Climbing roses, not yet in bloom, followed a trellis up the side of the gray shingles. The flower boxes were filled with blooming pansies, hyacinths, and daffodils. In a few weeks the island would celebrate the daffodil festival with an antique car parade and tailgating picnic, but the daffodils had decided to emerge a little early this year. A weathered gray bench sat opposite the door of the smaller cottage, perfect for looking out at the waves. A handheld movie camera sat on top of a vinyl case, an enormous lens jutting out of the front.

She walked up to the front door and knocked. "Hello?"

People on the other side of the door were arguing. She hefted the heavy brown-paper-wrapped package of books on her hip. Maybe now was a bad time. But, on the other hand, maybe now was the best of all possible times to interrupt them, before tempers rose even further. She knocked again.

The door flew open a few seconds later. Joe Carbonneau, the director, said, "May I help you?"

"Books for Al Petrillo."

He turned his head and shouted, "Al!" When no response came, he said, "Come in, why don't you?" and he stepped aside for her.

"Thank you for the coffee this morning," he said.

"Thank you for sending someone to get it."

"It was good coffee."

She kept a straight face, even though she had a sudden flash of Lance Mitchell shouting at her from the day before. "Thank you."

"Al!"

"Upstairs!" came the faint response.

"Books!"

"Right down!"

The director waved her toward a seat on a couch in the living room, in which several other people were sitting. None of them looked like movie stars. Angie recognized the set designer from before.

She sat next to the set designer, holding the brown paper package of books on her knees. She hoped that her hair wasn't too much of a mess from riding out to the B&B, but it was too late to do anything about it.

"You've heard," said the set designer. "About Lance."

Angie nodded. "A little. Detective Bailey came to ask questions this morning, but he didn't volunteer much information."

"He was found only this morning in his room at Jellicoe House, the B&B where some of the actors were staying. They think he might have been poisoned."

"Poisoned?" Angie asked.

"His airway swelled shut," the set designer said. "He choked to death. They're doing tests." The woman was staring at Angie in a pointed manner, as if to say, *Aren't you the island sleuth?*

Angie felt like making a run for it. "Has anyone been arrested?"

"No. Although I've heard that the bakery owners might be."

The question *did he have any enemies* waited on the tip of Angie's tongue. But it would have been a stupid question, even if she did feel like involving herself in an investigation of a famous Hollywood producer. Of course, Lance Mitchell had enemies.

Al Petrillo came down the stairs. "Where's that camera...?"

Angie stood up. "I just saw it outside. May I...?" She led him toward the door, grateful to escape.

Outside, Al swore at the camera briefly, as if it were a bad dog, then zipped it into the cover that had been resting underneath it. "Well, you just saved my butt," he said. "And you brought books! What did you bring me?"

They sat on the bench. Al unwrapped the paper, using a pocket knife to cut open the tape. "What's this...a new Walter Mosley! I didn't know he had a new one out. Ruth Ware, ah, and *Y is for Yesterday*, so sad that Sue Grafton died...*The Driver*? I haven't heard of that one. Hart Hanson."

"I haven't been able to read it yet," Angie said, with a slight blush. "It looked good, but it may not be."

"*Final Girls*...doesn't Universal have rights for that? I've heard some pretty big names associated with it."

"But you haven't read it yet, have you?"

"Yeah, I have." He flipped the book over and started scanning the back. "But who wouldn't love to film this, right?"

Before he could get lost in the book, something that had happened to Angie countless times herself, she said, "Al, can you tell me what's going on? Mickey and Jo Jerritt own the bakery where those cupcakes came from, and everyone's worried."

"Well, he was found dead in his room early this morning."

"How early?"

"Four thirty. They said he'd been dead for at least three hours."

*Who gets up at four thirty in the movie industry?* Angie wondered. "Was he with someone?"

"I don't know about that, but he was found by the fitness trainer. The actors can't afford to put on weight suddenly. Audiences freak out if your face has major changes during filming. So, we have a personal trainer with us. Mitchell insisted upon it. He was, you might say, a bit of a perfectionist."

Angie couldn't help but make a face.

Al put the book down and put a hand on her shoulder. "Hey. Don't stress it. Your coffee is plenty good, lady. It just ain't espresso from

Italy. He was the kind of guy who measured everything against perfection."

"I could do better."

He chuckled. "Let me correct myself. He was the kind of guy who measured everything *but himself* against perfection. Capiche?"

"Okay, so he was found by his fitness trainer at four-thirty this morning. What happened? How did he die?"

"They think he choked to death. But weird thing is, I heard he was found with this rash all over his body. Big, red lumps, crazy hives – the whole shebang. That's gotta be poison, right?" Al said.

They looked at each other. They were both mystery readers. The most common of poisons—in books at least—was cyanide.

Angie gasped. "Oh my god, Al. Think of any Agatha Christie novel. She uses cyanide as the weapon in practically *every* book. And it always gives the victim a rash."

Al nodded his head, seemingly mulling over the evidence.

"I'm not going to ask why it happened," Angie said. "I mean, it was obvious that the man had enemies."

"It's more of a mystery why he hadn't been murdered yet," Al agreed.

"But why *now*?" she asked. "What set off his killer?"

"What do you plan to do, give them a medal?" Al said. "Angie. Speaking as one book lover to another...don't get involved in this. Just don't. A real person did this. A real person who is still on the island, probably, and keeping a close eye on things to make sure their nice little murder goes unsolved. Don't be the person who gets in the way of whoever murdered the bigshot Hollywood producer."

She sighed. "You're right."

"That being said," he added, "maybe it was that explosion he had at you."

"That set off the killer?" she asked. "I don't understand. I didn't do it."

"Make sure you can prove that," Al said. "By the way, I have a favor to ask you."

"Oh?"

He handed her the copy of *Final Girls*. "Give this to Julia instead. Tell her I think she should read it. I think she'd be great as the main character."

Angie decided to drop the book off on her way back. She didn't *need* to, but honestly, she was feeling too nosy not to use the excuse to find out how Julia was taking Lance's death.

Jellicoe House was off Old South Road and was the kind of place where the tea was served with saucers. It was more posh than outright snobbish, but Angie always felt too paranoid to relax when she went inside. One of these days she was going to trip over a rug and smash into a ten-thousand-dollar display case, she just knew it.

She called Aunt Margery on the way over, saying that she would be late coming back to the store.

Aunt Margery said that it wouldn't be a problem. They said their goodbyes and hung up. Angie was suspicious. Surely Aunt Margery had heard about the confrontation with Dory Jerritt by then. In fact, Dory had probably called Aunt Margery to complain about it the moment she got back to her car. And yet Aunt Margery had said nothing about it.

Something was up.

As she parked the bike next to the building, she heard someone call her by name. "Ms. Prouty?"

Angie turned around in a circle, trying to see who had spoken. A figure was leaning from one of the upstairs windows. Lucy Smith. She called again, and Angie waved at her.

"I'll be right down," Ms. Smith said, closing the window.

Angie grabbed the book out of her basket and walked up to the front door, only to be nearly run over by Julia Withers.

"Oh!" Julia exclaimed, eyes wide. Her eyes were red and so was her nose. She looked like she'd been crying. "I didn't see you. But I'm glad I saw you. I mean, after I ran into you, I was glad. Not glad that I ran into you. I'm not glad that I ran into you, but I'm glad that I ran into you."

And then she threw her arms around Angie in an enormous hug and buried her face on Angie's shoulder, crying loudly.

Angie was surprised but not shocked. Weren't actresses supposed to be dramatic? Or was Julia overacting, trying to gain sympathy over Lance Mitchell's death? She patted Julia on the back and said, "Why don't we sit down, okay? I don't want to get run over by the next person coming through the door."

Julia laughed wetly, smearing tears and mascara on Angie's sleeve as she allowed Angie to lead her to a pair of armchairs nearby. Her hysteria seemed to be a bit too convenient, only bursting into tears again once Angie had seated her in the armchair. Angie put the book down, and Julia clutched her hand so tightly that it hurt.

"Are you okay?" Angie asked, after the new bout of tears had subsided somewhat.

"No!"

"I'm so sorry to hear about Lance, were you two close?"

Julia broke into a fresh bout of tears. Angie continued to hold her hand, while quickly glancing around the room. Where was Julia's assistant, Ms. Smith? Hadn't she just been coming downstairs? Why was the attendant at the cozy desk in the corner whispering into the phone and trying so obviously to not to pay attention?

They must not want to deal with Julia's tears any more than Angie did.

In between sobs, Julia said, "We were close. More than close, a long time ago. I met him at the Cannes Film Festival in France...we had a whirlwind romance...then as so many Hollywood romances do, it ended."

"So, you weren't together in recent history?"

"There was nothing," Julia wailed and waved her hands about as if to emphasize the point. Angie had a hard time pinning down whether Julia was just emotional in general or if there was more going on. She decided to take a chance to find out.

"It can be hard to let a love like that go. Did you think there was ever a chance you would get back together?"

"I wanted him to be the man I had met in France, the man I first started dating. But he refused. He said that he couldn't go back to being the man he used to be. He said he had grown too much for that. He said some ugly things to me."

"I'm so sorry," Angie said. Breaking up with Walter had been a cake walk by comparison. She wasn't sure what to do. Sit here with the woman as she had a mental breakdown? Try to convince her to go back to her room? Give her the audience she so clearly wanted?

A person appeared at the door holding a camera. Julia stiffened and quickly turned away. She stood up slowly, keeping her head turned, still gripping Angie's hand tightly. Julia turned and fled for the stairs, pulling Angie along behind her. At the last second, Angie remembered the book and stretched over to grab it.

Ms. Smith opened the door at the top of the stairs, let them in, then closed it and locked it behind her.

"I'm sorry, Julia, I didn't see them coming."

Julia Withers was shaking. "It's the press, isn't it? It's the press. The vultures have finally descended on this wonderful island."

The women peered out the window, leaving the lace curtains closed. Several white vans had just pulled into the parking lot. One of them had a Boston-area station logo on the side and a satellite dish on top.

"Oh, God," Julia said.

"Do you think they got anything?" Ms. Smith asked.

"I don't think so," Julia said, backing away from the window. "I kept my hair in front of my face. I *can't* cope with them now! Not now! Not ever!"

Ms. Smith turned slowly toward her boss. With a pitying look but a harsh tone of voice, she said, "Julia, you're better than this. You can handle this professionally. Without tears and snot covering your face, all right? A colleague has died. You don't know what happened. You weren't currently in a relationship with him. Investigations are ongoing. *You have no comment.* You *must* put on your armor. We've talked about this. Everyone acts. You're an *amazing* actress. You can fake your way through this. You don't need to be terrified of the press. You have this."

Julia's transformation took only a second. "Put on my armor. Right." If a moment ago she had been about to have a meltdown, she now seemed as though she would be competent enough to hold a press conference. Both Julia and Ms. Smith wore the same facial expression, and even had the same body posture. Angie suddenly realized that Julia was copying her assistant! They looked almost like sisters.

"Are you ready?"

"Ready?" Julia asked incredulously. "I'm not *ready* to discuss anything with the press. I'm not giving interviews, breaking down on camera, or answering questions. If they have questions, they can speak to the police."

"Good," Ms. Smith said. "But you're mimicking me again."

Julia's face turned into a panicked grimace. "I have to mimic someone, that's part of my armor." She looked over at Angie. "You seem like a level-headed woman, Angie, what would you do in my situation?"

Angie felt like saying, *Me? I'd stutter and panic!* but that was clearly not the answer that Julia needed at that moment. "I would do what I had to do to protect myself, my friends, and my bookstore."

Julia scrutinized her. "Say that again? Please?"

"Um...I'd do what I had to do to protect myself, my friends, and my bookstore?"

Julia adjusted how she stood, melting in to a pose that wasn't Lucy Smith's proud, straight bearing persona, and wasn't the hysterical ball of panic that she'd been a moment ago either. Angie made a face. Julia was imitating *her* now. Did she really slouch that much? Angie suddenly felt tired. She forced herself to stand up straight. Julia stood up straighter too, her expression falling into a kind of stubborn endurance.

Angie had to smile. She probably looked like that all the time. Too tired to cope, too stubborn to give up.

Julia smiled, too, this time not copying Angie. "People must like you."

"I guess so," Angie said. "I mostly like people, at any rate."

Julia reached out and gave Angie another hug. It was less awkward this time. "Okay. I can do this," she said. "I can borrow some bookstore owner stubbornness, some Hollywood assistant bitchiness, and some Daddy Withers charm and fake my way through this."

"What about just being Julia?" Angie asked. It was fascinating to watch Julia go through her changes, but it was also a little bit sad.

"Julia Withers has social anxiety and ADD and is going through the five stages of grief over an ex-lover who has been verbally abusive to her in the recent past," Julia said, as if talking about someone completely different. "Julia Withers needs about three days of binge-watching *Downton Abbey* and eating quarts of rocky road ice cream and going through about a dozen boxes of tissues, the lotion kind, because otherwise her nose will get chapped from so much crying. Julia Withers is a normal person who doesn't have to look good one hundred percent of the time, like, totally ready to be on TV. She can't handle this, and she doesn't want to. She doesn't want to take responsibility for any of this."

Julia looked at Ms. Smith. "But that's too bad, someone has to, so she's going to stand behind a façade and fake being able to handle this. She's going to finish filming. She's going to do such a good job at pretending to fall in love that you would never know that her heart feels like she will never love again."

Ms. Smith reached out and took Julia's hand.

"And when I get home," Julia said, "I'm going to cry over all the good things that Lance could have been, but wasn't, and I'm going to say goodbye. And then I'm going to go back to my parent's farm and hide for a month with their goats and their avocado trees." Angie was surprised that such a glamorous Hollywood celebrity had farmers for parents.

She looked down. Angie was still holding the book. "Oh! *Final Girls*. Al Petrillo, I don't know if you know him, he's a cameraman, says that you should read this and that you should audition for the lead, if they ever make it into a movie." Julia took the book out of Angie's hand, flipped to the first page, and started to read.

Angie felt a moment of sympathy...for Lucy Smith, who had to keep track of her boss and her mental state *all the time*. It must be exhausting.

After a brief consultation with Lucy about what to do next, Angie called the bookstore to tell Aunt Margery that she was going out with Julia and Ms. Smith for a meal, either an afternoon snack or an early supper, whatever it was called. There was nothing like grief to give someone an appetite, and Julia was starving. She had been eating at Nonatum's because it was close and because it was where all the actors were eating. When Sheldon had come by the set with lobster roll samples, they had all been delighted—but she hadn't had a chance to eat there yet.

Aunt Margery said that the store was quiet, and that Mickey had stopped by to check on the pastry status. He had seemed disappointed not to be able to talk to her in person.

"Was it something important?" Angie asked.

"He wouldn't say."

"I'll call him to tell him that we'll be at Shelly's," Angie said. "I don't think anyone would mind the extra company...I wonder if Jo wants to come, too?"

"Her young gentleman has arrived on the island to lavish her with all due care and tenderness," Aunt Margery said. "She left a message saying not to worry if you weren't able to reach her. Something about loud music and steel-toed boots at an underground club in Boston."

Detective Bailey had almost certainly told Jo and Mickey not to leave the island during the investigation. Angie laughed and said, "Teddy is the perfect gentleman...for Jo, anyway. I'll call Mickey and tell him. Thank you."

"Have a good time. There's a few things I'll leave for you to finish up at the store, but don't hurry back, dear, Janet and I have it covered."

She still wasn't saying anything about Dory. Or about investigating the murder.

What was Aunt Margery up to?

## Chapter 8

## THE SLEUTH

Sheldon's Shuckery was one of those places that gets described as being over the top, larger than life, and more wonderful than the describer can accurately describe. First-time visitors will usually think, "What's the big deal?"

From the outside the Shuckery didn't look like much.

The building had started out as a tiny cottage back in the early nineteen hundreds. The owners had come into some money and built an expansion onto the cottage. Their family had expanded, and the cottage had grown again. Then, one of the grandchildren of the original owners had decided to go into business serving fresh fish to travelers. With the house's location overlooking the harbor and the wharf, it was an ideal place to obtain the freshest fish, right off the boats. The building had expanded again, taking over a couple of houses along the block.

As a result, the building didn't look like it had been planned so much as grown, like moss on a tree. It was *not* the most elegant building on

Nantucket. In the front of a building was a small parking lot with too few spaces. The overflow parking was an unmarked gravel lot across the street, with cars jamming in at crazy angles during high tourist season.

Sheldon loved to collect antiques, so every window was stuffed with shelves full of dusty, ancient glass bottles. The curtains were all at least sixty years old and didn't match from window to window. The purple paint on the trim was peeling, and the carved wooden signs advertised everything from fuel oil to marinas on the mainland. Rusty junk sat in corners, separated from the cars by rope-and-post fences. The only sign that the place wasn't just some crazy antique store was the one on the front door giving the actual name of the restaurant and the business hours.

And the smell.

To walk within three blocks of Sheldon's Shuckery was to have your stomach start to growl and your mouth start to water.

Angie directed the driver of the VW Microbus that had come to get them to drop them off by the door. Mickey had said that he would meet up with them after a while. He had a few things to wrap up at the bakery. The two other women had peered through the Microbus's windows at the building. Being a Monday, the parking lot wasn't full. Angie recognized Shelly's old blue Ford truck, looking like a rusty bulldog in the parking lot.

"Are you sure this is the right place?" Julia asked.

"Wait for it," Angie assured her. The driver got out and opened the door for them, and they all climbed out.

Julia stopped on the sidewalk, rocking back on her heels. "I don't know what that smell is, but it's good."

Ms. Smith had an even stronger reaction. She made a face that was almost near tears. "This smells...oh, this smells like my grandmother's house."

Angie said, "Tell that to Jeanette and she will love you forever."

She led them inside, where Sheldon quickly spotted them. "Ladies!" he exclaimed. "Any guests of Miss Angie are favorite guests of mine."

Sheldon was a short, solidly built man with what could only be described as a homely face. He looked like he could be the ugly bartender in a movie set in Mexico in 1850. His skin was like leather that hadn't been well cared for and his fingers were gnarled.

"Shelly," Angie said, "This is Julia Withers from the set of the movie, and her assistant Lucy Smith. They haven't eaten here before."

There was a whole conversation hidden away in that statement: *The star of the movie has been eating at a competitor's restaurant that shall not be named, but please don't hold it against them, they didn't know any better!*

Sheldon chuckled to himself. "Well, they will not want to eat anywhere else, now!"

"There have been some paparazzi trying to interview Julia," Angie said.

"Say no more," he interrupted her. "Uncle Shelly will make sure that the princesses aren't found by the evil photographers. Leave it to me."

He escorted them to a table in the back of the house. They had to take three different hallways to reach it. Angie had no fear of being ignored, though, their table was right by the kitchen.

"Thanks, Shelly."

"Anything to start?"

"Please," Angie said. She had already checked to make sure that neither of the women were allergic to anything.

After Sheldon had left, Julia leaned forward. "You didn't tell him what we wanted."

Angie grinned. "We don't want what the tourists want. We want whatever Sheldon and Jeanette decide to bring us."

The appetizer turned out to be smoked bluefish pâté with tiny rye toasts, capers, pickled red onions, fresh thyme, and paper-thin slices of green apple.

Lucy explained that her grandmother was from Québec, although she had been raised in Burbank, California. The meal was similar to food she had been raised on. Lucy took about a hundred photos with her camera, starting with shots of the food, mentioning that she couldn't wait to show her grandmother. Eventually she was turning and twisting around in her chair, trying to get a look at everything. Even in the back of the restaurant, every surface was packed with antiques.

In the corner, a fake shark's mask covered the head of a fashion mannequin wearing a beaded flapper dress. A porcelain panther guarded a shelf full of pewter dragons with faceted crystal eyes. A gigantic, hazy mirror whose frame was covered with pocket watches reflected a huge wooden sign that looked like it was written in Greek. A tin sign next to it read *We're Happy as Clams!* One section of the wall was hung with smashed guitars and banjos. Underneath it, a brass fireplace fan showed off its shiny peacock feathers.

Julia said, "You could never use this place for location shooting. It's too distracting."

"It's wonderful," Lucy said.

"That's true, too," Julia said.

After they had demolished the pâté, Jeanette arrived to take the rest of their order. Things at Sheldon's didn't always work like they did at regular restaurants, especially if Sheldon and Jeanette liked you.

Jeanette was the kind of tall, elegant Frenchwoman that makes American women tear their hair out in jealousy. She always seemed effortlessly stylish yet casual, as if the hours that other women had to spend on their hair and makeup and fashion would never replace the true beauty given to her through her innate Parisian confidence.

"Hello, sweet child," she said, kissing Angie on her cheeks. "Friends of yours?"

"New ones," Angie said. "They're with the movie."

"Ah, *oui*," Jeanette said. "Poor Lance, no?"

Something about the way Jeanette said his name, made Angie remember her conversation with Carol back at the Chamber of Commerce.

"You knew him?" Angie asked incredulously. *What were the odds?*

"I did, although that was a very long time ago, in France. He was part of the scene with all the young filmmakers then. A fan of the moviemaker Jean-Luc Goddard, especially. He was a good boy then, *très beau*. But I think he was always sad that he wasn't born earlier, in the days of the great innovators whom he admired. I said, 'Lance, you must become one of the great innovators, you surely have it in you to become a great *auteur*.' But he didn't believe that he could do it. He tried to make films, and they all disgusted him. He tried to write the screenplays, and they disgusted him, too. 'What else can I do?' he cried. 'Give it time,' I said. We all liked his films, even though he hated them himself. But then he became a producer, and had much more success bringing the films of others to life. *Mon Dieu*... It seems like ages ago now, but yes. Lance and I were friends.'"

"So, I suppose it's no coincidence that he came to produce here on the island?" Angie asked, curious.

"Well, no," Jeanette shrugged her shoulders. "After I left Paris, I always told Lance how beautiful Nantucket is. I even emailed Lance just last year, telling him as much. I never heard back from him, but I suppose he received the email, because... well, you know." Jeanette had tears in her eyes and looked away from Angie.

Angie peered over at Lucy and Julia, but they had clammed up. "Lance seemed very angry when I met him."

"*Oui*. You would be angry, too, if you had suppressed the talents that you had been given instead of using them. He should have become an *auteur*. Instead he used his talents to make other people's work better. He was always pushing his *auteurs* to become better."

"How did you meet him?" Angie asked.

"It was at a film festival. I was dating a boy who was a director. It was a little festival, not one of the great ones, but the French are mad for the cinema. It is everywhere. There are more film theaters in Paris than there are in New York, in practically all of America I think! It is a great pastime of ours."

"Were you a cook then?" Angie asked, curious.

"*Non*, not a cook. I had thought I would become a screenwriter. But it was just a thought. I didn't enjoy it at all. I would get up in the middle of a monologue to make an omelet, or to run out to the street to get a crepe from my favorite cart, and then I would talk to the owner for a long time. He would say, 'Jeanette, I must run an errand, will you make the crepes for me?' And I would. It was such a pleasure. But of course, that boyfriend, he had such plans for us. I would write the scripts, and he would make the movies. I didn't like to tell him that I didn't want to write for anyone, I wanted to roast chickens and makes pommes frites instead." She laughed. "I met Sheldon after that. He was in Paris to become a screenwriter as well, you know, living poor in a garret in Paris with a typewriter and a magnificent sense of injustice, as though it was after the Second World War and he was Hemingway. We all met and exchanged our screenplays for critique with each other, and then, one day out of the blue after a bad critique, he asked me to run away with him to America and cook food instead. I thought, 'How did he know of my secret passion? It must be true love.' And we have been together ever since."

The women smiled. Julia said, "I think Lance mentioned you once."

"Oh?"

"He didn't mention you by name, but he did say that he had once been told by one of the most beautiful women in the world that he was meant to make movies, but that all that meant was that beautiful Frenchwomen were not to be trusted."

Jeanette flashed a quick smile, but her eyes looked sad. "He should have trusted me. He would not be dead if he had."

Angie asked, "Why do you say that?"

"If he had made movies, he would have been happy," Jeanette said. "People who are murdered are not happy people."

Angie thought about that. Alexander Snuock, Walter's father, had been murdered; he had definitely been unhappy. Her friend Reed Edgerton, who had been murdered last year, had been content with his life, though. He had just been in the wrong place at the wrong time.

As if Jeanette had been reading her mind, she reached over and patted Angie's hand. "Not always, though. Sometimes they are merely people who have been crushed by fate. You should not blame yourself for Reed's death."

"I feel like I attract that kind of thing, now," Angie said.

Jeanette said, "Who knows? Maybe you do. But someone needs to care about these things, whether the persons involved were pleasant or otherwise."

"What do you mean, Jeanette?"

Jeanette rolled her eyes as if she were explaining chocolate to a toddler. "I mean you solved those murders, Angie. Everyone knows this. You care, and you are good at it. It's good to do."

"You're saying I should quit my job as a bookseller and start up a private detective agency?" Angie said sarcastically.

"Oh, no, don't do that! Who would pick out books for me?" Jeanette laughed. "Here I am talking to you. How hungry you must be! What would you like to eat?"

Angie told her to pick whatever she felt like. Julia said she wanted a lobster roll.

Lucy said, "My grandmother was French Canadian, and your restaurant smells like her kitchen. I want you to make me remember her."

"Do you have a favorite dish?"

"Beef with onions and morel mushrooms."

"*Daube de bœuf.* That is a stew that takes a long time, *ma chère.* Come back tomorrow, and I will have it for you. Today, I will think of what to bring you that you will like. You can trust me."

Julia excused herself to the restroom. Angie decided to try to get more information out of her assistant while she was gone.

"Is Julia all right?" she asked Lucy.

Lucy shook her head. She had taken her hair out of its prim bun. It lay on her shoulders. She would look much more attractive if she just loosened up a little, Angie decided.

"Lance and Julia got in a horrible fight the night before he died," Lucy said. "I had gone over to the little kitchenette to make hot water for chamomile tea when I heard them in Julia's room at about eleven."

Jellicoe House had, at one point, sometime around the 1850's, been a rooming house for single, often widowed women, and had a shared kitchenette upstairs that guests were allowed to use.

Angie said, "What about?"

"Whenever Lance and Julia meet, they have a fight. It's just expected."

"What did they fight about?" Angie was hoping to get something specific from Lucy.

Lucy shrugged. "The usual, I suppose. He wanted to sleep with her, no strings attached, and she wanted to have a relationship. You don't need to hear it to know what it's about. They tell each other to grow up and shout some more."

"Were they in love?"

"No," Lucy said without hesitation. "He wanted to think he was in lust and didn't care, and she wanted to think she was in love, and did. But I think all that had been over for a long time. They weren't even friends."

"That's sad."

"Sometimes people hang on for far too long and make each other miserable."

Angie sighed. "If you want to hear the not-too-tragic story of how I broke up with my last boyfriend, so it didn't drag on past the point where we were still interested in each other, just say so. But please don't."

Lucy flashed her a sweet smile. "Don't feel bad about not wanting to talk about it. Not everyone needs to be a professional drama queen...I mean actress."

Julia came back down the hallway from the restroom, trailing a much taller companion. It was Mickey.

"I found the baker!" Julia said triumphantly.

"Hey, Angie," Mickey said, seating himself at their table with Angie on one side and Lucy on the other, so he could face Julia the movie star. "You started without me, didn't you?"

"Of course," Angie said.

"You still haven't forgiven me for that one time in eighth grade." He had kept an entire table of eighth-graders waiting for an hour for him on their final day of middle school.

She rolled her eyes. "You *told* me you were going to be late tonight."

"I didn't *mean* you could *eat* without me," he said, copying her tone.

"Fine. Next time I'll starve."

"Yeah. You'll just waste away." He put the back of his hand to his forehead and pretended to faint. She snorted.

"How did it go today?" she asked.

"Craptastic!" he said. "It's amazing how a police investigation can throw off your whole day."

"Tell me about it," she said.

He did, recounting the story of being suspected of murdering Lance Mitchell so amusingly that he had Lucy and even Julia laughing at him. Angie surreptitiously rubbed her cheeks when he had finished, she had been smiling so much. Mickey could always get a grin out of her.

He turned to Julia and Lucy. "So that was my day. How did your day go? I heard you lost a producer?"

Lucy said, "He was quite the production, all right."

"But was he productive?" Mickey asked.

"Practically."

"So, the practically productive producer has paid the ultimate price," Mickey said. "He has pegged out."

Angie shook her head. Listening to the two of them was like listening to Katherine Hepburn and Spencer Tracy riff off each other. But Julia's face had gone stiff. She'd better derail the two of them cracking jokes about Julia's ex's death.

"Mickey, have you ordered yet?"

"I saw Sheldon on the way in. I just told him to feed me. He said, and I quote, "that I had to pay for everyone's meals.""

"What?" Angie asked.

"Not with money. With an idea. He wants a new dessert, something that'll knock people's socks off. And," Mickey raised a hand, "before you ask me why he doesn't just ask Jeanette, he said, 'She's a cook, not a baker. Don't worry. We've talked about this together and we'd both like you to do it.'"

"So, you're going to start providing desserts for Sheldon's?" Angie asked.

"Sounds like it."

"Super," Lucy said.

Angie rolled her eyes. It was a bad idea to encourage Mickey to make puns and crack jokes. It really was. But at least it was on a different topic than Lance Mitchell's murder.

"I think that you should run with this," Angie said. "Don't just come up with one dessert. Take over making *all* their desserts – more for me to enjoy," Angie added with a grin.

"Hmm, what specific desserts would you have me make, Ms Prouty?"

"Cinnamon buns. Make sure you always bake some of those. I love them." Angie's mind flashed back to the gooey, sticky cinnamon buns that her mom used to make when she, Jo, and Mickey were young.

Mickey smiled. "I know you do. Except cinnamon buns are for breakfast, those aren't desserts, but that's an argument for another time." Mickey's eyes flickered over the table to Angie. He cleared his throat. "Anyway, what dessert could possibly scream 'Sheldon's Shuckery'? Oyster cake?"

"That would make people scream, all right," Lucy said.

Mickey turned to her and waggled his eyebrows. "That's what *she* said," he said suggestively. Then he turned back to Angie. "I kind of want to branch out from cupcakes. I love coming up with new flavor combos, but it's kind of a drag not being able to work on anything but cupcakes, cupcakes, cupcakes."

"And pastries," Angie said. "Don't forget you owe me pastries."

"Don't worry. I won't abandon the store," Mickey said.

As if she'd been deeply meditating on the subject, Julia said, "What about whoopie pies? Those are cupcakes with the frosting in the middle. If I didn't have to stay on my diet I would eat about a million of those. Or macarons."

"Brown sugar pie," Lucy said.

"Maple-walnut cake," said Angie.

"Salted chocolate pudding cakes," Julia said. Her eyes had glazed over. "You know what I want? I want a chocolate ooey gooey bar dripping with marshmallow fluff."

"What about tiny desserts?" Angie said. "Mix and match dessert shooters, something like that?"

"I'll think about it," Mickey said as he stretched. "Oh, man. I have to admit that it was less stressful being interviewed by Detective Bailey this morning than it was dealing with Lance Mitchell yesterday. He came in, bought a half-dozen cupcakes, and gave me a bunch of backhanded compliments about how great my cupcakes were, compared to every other bakery on Nantucket."

"Ouch," Angie said. There weren't any other bakeries on Nantucket.

"Yeah. He offered to help set up a business out in L.A., though." He stretched out one hand and made a rainbow-shaped gesture overhead. "Baker to the stars. All I had to do was abandon Nantucket, survive my sister's death threats, and learn how to compete with people ten times as good as I was, he said. What a favor, right?"

"Jo would absolutely kill you."

Mickey grinned. "She would. Which was the only part of the plan that actually sounded appealing."

Lucy said, "I wouldn't mind seeing more of you in L.A."

"You'd see me tear my hair out," Mickey said. "I'm an islander. I like not being able to hop over to the mainland all the time. There are too many people on the mainland. Okay, admittedly there are tourists on the island, but they tend to go away again after a while. Like, for months at a time. Although the season's kind of sneaking up on us now." He sighed dramatically. "Soon, it will be like ants at a picnic."

"Oreo cheesecake," Julia said.

"It's been done," Mickey said.

"Poke cake," Angie said.

"Ugh, not poke cake," Mickey said. "Lime Jell-O. Just no. Mom used to make that all the time. I'm still sick of it."

"Doesn't have to be Lime Jell-O. It could be, I don't know, rum cream or something."

"There's a thought. I can't do alcohol at the bakery, that's just not what we do, but I could totally get away with it at Sheldon's." Mickey hummed to himself under his breath.

A pair of servers appeared with a mountain of food, including raw oysters, duck confit with grilled peaches, swordfish à la niçoise, bouillabaisse, seared fluke, and more. There were even sardine tartines with tomato paste. Lucy fought Mickey for the last one with an arm-wrestling match, which Mickey pointedly lost.

It was a feast, and the four of them ate and drank until they were groaning.

"How can anyone even think about dessert after something like that?" Angie asked.

"There's *always* room for dessert," Mickey said.

Lucy giggled. "That's what *he* said."

As they laughed, Angie realized that Lucy was flirting with Mickey. She had, in fact, been flirting with him all night. Angie normally took Mickey so much for granted that she had completely missed it. Angie felt a wave of envy wash over her. She blushed, a little tipsy and more than a little embarrassed by her feelings.

Sheldon was serious about making Mickey brainstorm brilliant dessert ideas for him; none of them were presented with a bill. They left money to tip their servers and stumbled out into the dark.

Angie had a moment of panic as she realized that she'd abandoned Aunt Margery with the store all day. Then she reminded herself that Aunt Margery had not expected her to come back to the store before closing. Janet was there too - it would be fine. Tomorrow was Tuesday and they were closing the store for the day. Aunt Margery had become very strict about making sure Angie took a day off.

"Would you like me to walk you ladies home?" Mickey asked.

But the VW Microbus had just pulled up to pick them up.

Lucy looked directly at Mickey and said, "You're welcome to have a lift anywhere with us."

Angie thought Lucy had dropped Mickey a not-to-subtle hint. She felt surprisingly jealous by the flirting.

Mickey just waved. "No, I'm good, beautiful evening for a walk. Have a good night!" He turned and smiled at Angie, shrugging.

The bus drove off. True to Sheldon's word, they had managed to completely escape a confrontation with the paparazzi.

Mickey and Angie found themselves walking along Harbor View Way out of Sheldon's parking lot, in no real hurry to get anywhere, with the sound of the waves on the Children's Beach providing a soothing background hush.

"I think Lucy likes you," she said.

"Ah, she's not for me. She's a big-city girl. Are you going home or to the bookstore?"

"The bookstore, of course."

They turned at the corner.

"Hey, sorry about my mom," he said. "I heard that the two of you had a confrontation earlier today."

"It irritates me that people just expect me to solve their problems for them," Angie said. "Ugh. Carol Brightwell managed to imply that it was my civic duty. Kind of like, 'Don't let this murder hurt tourism!' As if scandal would actually drive people away. It just attracts them."

"True," he agreed. They turned again, this time away from the bookstore. By unspoken agreement they were headed across Children's Beach toward Steamboat Wharf, where all the ferries came in.

"Forgive me for pointing this out," he said, "but it seems like you're investigating the murder anyway. Isn't that why you were hanging out with Lucy and Julia?"

The wind got stronger as they climbed up onto the wharf. The last of the ferries had come in, but there was still one, a Hy-Line, waiting to go out. The passengers were loaded and ready to go.

"I don't know," Angie said. "I was determined to keep my nose out of things this time, but coincidence seems to be carrying me closer."

"Well, do you *want* to investigate? Or have you talked yourself out of it?"

"I keep thinking that I shouldn't," she admitted. Ticking each item on her fingers, she said, "It's dangerous. It's none of my business. Detective Bailey isn't an idiot. It just stirs up trouble with people. This murder, in particular, could get me into big trouble, since it involves someone kinda famous. The guy that was murdered not only didn't have any connection to me, but really got under my skin. I'm not the kind of person who runs around saying, 'Justice must be done.' And... honestly, I think your mom is just freaking out. You're not seriously being considered as a suspect, are you?"

"Ah..." Mickey said. "I get the feeling that if they don't catch someone soon, the investigation is going to shift to the bakery. I'm waiting for someone to say that we accidentally added something to the cupcakes."

"Poison?" Angie asked.

"They don't know for sure that it's poison yet."

"Lucy described what Lance's trainer saw when she found him. It sounds a lot like cyanide poisoning."

"That's some pretty indirect evidence," Mickey said.

"See? That's why I shouldn't be butting in on murder cases," Angie said. "I don't know what I'm doing, not really."

"You could find out," Mickey pointed out. "Why not? You read fast enough. Take a couple of days to read all the forensics books you can find. Bam! Now you're an expert on criminal investigations. Or at least not a complete ignoramus."

"It's not the same thing. And I could be legally liable for all kinds of things. I have no idea what, though."

"Are you breaking any laws?"

"I don't know, and I don't actually know how to find out."

"You could look it up online. You could even get a private detective license."

Angie blew air out of her cheeks. "It sounds like a lot of work for something I'm not sure I want to get involved in. And how many murder cases are going to happen on Nantucket, anyway?"

"'If you build it, they will come,'" Mickey said, quoting *Field of Dreams*, a cheesy old baseball movie.

"Wouldn't that be horrible?"

"Jessica Fletcher worshipped dark forces," he said. "She killed all those people in *Murder She Wrote*."

"What are you even talking about, dark forces?" she asked.

"Jessica Fletcher. The writer who investigated all the murders in her small town? Don't tell me you don't recognize the reference."

"Sure, and I've even heard the fan theory that she was the real murderer the whole time, although I don't buy it, *having actually seen all the episodes*. She couldn't have done them all; it wasn't physically possible in a lot of the cases."

"She had the help of supernatural forces," Mickey said in a booming, ominous tone that made several people standing along the rail of the ferry turn to look at them.

She punched him gently in the shoulder. "Mickey! Keep it down."

"There's probably an online forum somewhere for amateur sleuths now, too," Mickey said. "That's how I'd do it. A network of sleuths who know their local hunting grounds but who team up together to hunt murderers. No one can escape!"

She rolled her eyes.

"Hey," he said, "at least it would make for a great book."

"I don't want to be the island's local sleuth, and I don't want to be the local crime writer. I just want to be the local bookstore owner."

"You can keep telling yourself that, but you are good at getting to the bottom of things, Angie." Mickey said.

"You mean that?" Angie asked as she looked into his eyes.

"Yeah, of course. Angie you are great. You are smart, you understand people, you ask the right questions, you make all the right logical connections. You're... special."

"Mickey, thanks, that's... really sweet."

"Hey, you're shivering," he said.

She hadn't really noticed how cold it had become. She also hadn't really planned anything other than going out to the Island Harmony B&B earlier that afternoon. She was wearing a long-sleeved shirt and a canvas vest, but the air had become much colder, almost freezing.

Mickey pulled off his jacket, a brightly colored, overstuffed down coat, and reached down to put it over Angie's shoulders. Mickey's hand brushed against her own as she turned to grab the jacket from him. The two awkwardly blushed.

"Thanks, but really. I'm fine," she said.

"Don't be fine," he said. "Be warm."

"You aren't cold?"

"Watching you shiver is just going to make me uncomfortable. Take it."

She put it on. They had walked all the way to the end of the wharf, and the breeze was stiff. Mickey crossed his arms over his button-up shirt—he had probably avoided dressing in one of his usual informal t-shirts because he knew Julia and Lucy would be there—and exhaled heavily.

"What's the matter?"

He looked at her, then back toward the water. "I don't know. I just have a bad feeling about all this. Like, the bakery getting closed by health inspectors and losing my shirt kind of bad feeling about all this."

"What do you think really happened?" Angie asked. "That he just died accidentally?"

"No, a guy like that had to have been murdered," he said. "I mentioned when he bought them that we can't guarantee to be peanut-free and he didn't say anything, so I don't think that was it either. Cyanide? Who puts cyanide in a cupcake?"

"Everyone knew he had a sweet tooth."

"So, who would you call as suspects? Besides me and Jo, obviously."

"Julia for sure. They got in a fight the night before, a real screaming match. And she seems so mercurial that I can't tell whether she's actually sad or just acting like it. Maybe Lucy, because she seems both very defensive of Julia, and wound up too tightly. I can see her losing her temper, but I don't see her as a poisoner. I think she would have beat Lance to death if she had been the one to snap."

"Agreed," Mickey said. "I mean, who poisons someone? It's in all the mysteries because it's a convenient way to widen the circle of suspects, but sheesh. Just cold-bloodedly putting poison into a cupcake. What if the wrong person ate it by accident? And wouldn't you want to be there to see it? I mean, if you're going to poison someone, it's because you want them dead, I'm assuming. So, wouldn't you want to be there, like, 'Hahaha, I will have my revenge' kind of thing?"

"It isn't always revenge. Maybe it's Al Petrillo. Or the director. If one of them wanted to take over the production for some reason. One of them has to be in charge now. Who benefits? That's the question."

"I think you're just running down all the people you've met from the movie set and trying them on for size."

"You're right," Angie said, feeling embarrassed. "I'll knock it off."

Mickey didn't say anything else about the bakery or the murder. He seemed to shake off his blue mood for her sake, telling her funny stories about bakery customers he'd had lately. They reached the bookstore where Aunt Margery was just closing up. They could see her through the back window.

Mickey said, "I guess this is goodbye, then."

"How can I say goodbye if you keep turning up like a bad penny?"

"You know, that saying was a lot funnier before I had to count up the change in a cash drawer every day."

She pulled his jacket off. Mickey's jacket didn't smell like Walter's. Walter always smelled like expensive cologne. Mickey's jacket smelled like Old Spice mixed with powdered sugar; unique and comforting. She handed it over, and Mickey put it back on, holding it close to his chest. "Whew."

"Cold?"

"Yeah, you smell good," he said, sniffing the inside of the lapel. "Like old books. Too bad guys can't ask to borrow girl's clothing the way girls do guys' clothing."

Angie found herself giggling. "Picturing you trying on one of my jackets is a pretty funny image."

"Well, we'll have to try it sometime."

She laughed again, and Mickey moved in closer to give her a hug goodnight.

"Night, Angie." He whispered.

"Good night Mickey." She looked up at him as he hugged her, breathing in that Old Spice one more time.

Angie watched as Mickey's tall frame ambled away. After a few feet he turned back and gave her another goofy wave and a smile before turning the corner and disappearing from her sight.

Angie found herself standing outside the bookstore thinking about Mickey, and how her feelings for him might be changing.

"What just happened there?" Asked Aunt Margery, appearing out of nowhere.

Angie was startled.

"What do you mean? Nothing really, Mickey just walked me home."

"Didn't seem like nothing to me." Aunt Margery said as she gently pulled Angie into the store and out of the cold, "If you'd waited ten more minutes I'd have locked the door and gone."

Angie gave her a hug. "Thank you so much for watching the store."

"Have a good time?"

Angie gave her a quick rundown of the day's events, not skipping over her confrontation with Dory or the fact that Mickey had completely missed Lucy Smith trying to hit on him, and recounting the major points discussed during dinner.

Aunt Margery took it all in, asking only a few questions.

As Angie spoke, she found herself getting more and more frustrated by the murder. "Why, Aunt Margery? Why do things like this have to happen? Why do people decide that they have to do something like this?"

Aunt Margery shrugged. "'All the motives for murder are covered by four Ls: Love, Lust, Lucre and Loathing.' P.D. James, *The Murder Room*."

"I have never really believed that quote," Angie said. "What, that's it? What about road rage? Serial killers? School shooters? What about John Hinckley, Jr., trying to assassinate Ronald Reagan so he could impress Jodie Foster? That wasn't love or lust, it was a temper tantrum. And what about accidents where the person involved doesn't really set out to murder someone, but things escalate?"

Aunt Margery spread her hands out. "In many ways, I'm not fit to be a detective, Agatha. I want real life to end up being something that won't upset me too much. I want to be comfortable. I want to see people's flaws, but I also want to downplay those flaws. I'm a terrible gossip, I know, but I'm also the first one to downplay the wrongness that I see in people and turn it into a mere quirk."

Angie said, "I can't do that."

"I know. When you see the worst in people, you never let yourself forget it. For better or worse."

"I feel like I both wish I could understand what makes murderers really tick, and really grateful that I don't," Angie said.

"Sometimes we are given gifts that we don't especially want to receive," Aunt Margery said. "By a higher power, by fate, or even just by evolution, I can't say. But they remain gifts, and if we don't use them, we risk becoming less than our true selves."

"What do you mean? What gifts do you have?" Angie asked.

"I hold people together," Aunt Margery said. "Sometimes, I hold them together from a very, very long way away. I don't just gossip, dear, I smooth ruffled feathers, negotiate compromises, and make suggestions on how to handle people who are behaving irrationally."

Angie laughed. "I would be terrible at that!"

Aunt Margery slipped an arm around her waist and gave her a hug. "So you would. I'm so glad that you've finally decided to appreciate what I do."

"I probably don't fully appreciate what you do," she said, hugging her great-aunt back. "Someday, though, I will. Tonight, I think I'll just finish up a few things around here and then go to bed," Angie said.

"Remember, we are *closing* the store tomorrow," Aunt Margery said.

"Yes, and I plan to come in and do some adjusting on the espresso machine," Angie said.

Aunt Margery patted Angie's hand with a sigh. "You will stay out of the store tomorrow. For sanity's sake. Take the day off. Do some reading. You remember books? You used to read them."

"I still read them."

"But now you're going to take an entire day to read them, instead of skimming them in the back of the store for fifteen minutes at a time."

"I do *not* skim. I speed read." Angie's mind suddenly flashed back to her conversation with Mickey. Out of the blue, the thing she hadn't wanted to talk to her great-aunt about came spilling out. "Oh, Aunt Margery. Mickey's worried that they'll try to blame Lance Mitchell's death on him and the bakery. I don't know what to do."

"I think you do," she said. "Find out what happened. Give the information discreetly to Detective Bailey. Let him take all the credit publicly."

"But I don't want to become the Nantucket sleuth. It's ridiculous."

"Don't become a sleuth, then. Become a student of human nature."

"Like Miss Marple? That's like becoming the crazy cat lady, only worse. I'm never going to have a real boyfriend. I already have this sign on my head that says, *don't bother, extremely nosy small bookseller and amateur sleuth.* I'm going to die alone. An old maid."

Aunt Margery said, "All done complaining?"

"No. Yes. For now."

"Tomorrow. Books. Rest. Sleep in. Recharge. Turn off the phone if you have to."

"And then?"

"And then consider, if you will, the best use of the talents you have been given. Don't dwell on what you think other people will think of you. You don't get to decide who will look down upon you or reject you, or even feel gratitude toward you for saving him from a murder trial, and then become bored with you because you have responsibilities that *he* never had."

"Aunt Margery!"

"The word you've been using to describe what you do, *sleuth*, tells only a tiny piece of the story. It no more sums you up than *old maid* describes me."

Angie's shoulders slumped. "I'm sorry. I wasn't thinking. I didn't mean it."

"You judge yourself more harshly than you judge me. Do people around the island call me an old maid?"

"I don't know. Not to my face, anyway."

"My life is more than the words *old maid* and *gossip*, Angie. Just as your life is worth more than the words *bookseller* or even *amateur sleuth*."

Chapter 9

# THINGS GET WORSE

Angie lived with her great-aunt in a cottage near downtown that was worth a ridiculous amount of money and which had to be the most adorable cottage in the entire world. It was two stories with only one large room at the top—Angie's bedroom. Downstairs was Aunt Margery's room, one storage-slash-guest room, one big living-slash-dining room, a modest kitchen, and a tiny utility room. Underneath the house was a crawl space - a dark, terrible, and spider-webby place that Angie had to venture into once a year to change the furnace filters.

Angie's grandparents had passed a while ago, and her parents, who were known as members of the traveling Proutys, the ones who became whaling captains and traveling salesmen in previous generations, were currently running some weird type of hotel down in Florida.

Angie and her great-aunt were the other kind of Proutys, the staying Proutys. They were the ones who left home for a short time, but ended up coming back to the island, content to put down their oilskin bags and steamer trunks and spend the rest of their lives never really going anywhere else.

Angie had initially left the island to become a financial analyst in Manhattan. She had traveled to Europe, South Africa, and even Japan for her job. It wasn't that she didn't think the world was worth seeing; it was just that everywhere she had been had felt like a quick fling, lasting a month or a week or even a single night. Even Manhattan had grown stale. Back to Nantucket she had come with fresh eyes. The island that had felt like a prison when she was a teenager now felt like heaven.

However, Walter hadn't been ready to settle down with her, either romantically or with Nantucket as his home. That was obvious.

As Angie walked through the cottage, she would sometimes have to just stop to admire how perfect, how wonderful, and how charming it was. It was decorated with books, of course, every wall lined with built-in shelves. There were so many books that they had recently started turning them sideways to jam them in. It wasn't quite to the level of towers of books teetering on the couch cushions, but it was close.

Angie wandered along the shelves, and shelves, and shelves of books, most of which she wouldn't dream of giving up. However, most of the books were also books that she had read before, and she didn't want to reread any of them especially. Not today. Today was a day for new adventures, new murders, and new romances.

The island library, called the Nantucket Atheneum, a white-columned building with creaking wood floors, spindly chairs in the corner, and stately hardbacks on every shelf, would be a wonderful place to visit today.

It opened at nine-thirty a.m.

Four hours from now.

The curse of the early riser had struck again; Angie was up far before the rest of the world was ready to do more than slap the alarm and roll over in their sleep.

She would just sneak over to the store for a moment to pick out some books. Aunt Margery would never know she had been there. Captain Parfait needed to be fed, anyway.

Perusing the shelves, Angie selected a small stack of books. She sat down in her chair in the back of the store and opened one. She'd just read a page or two to see if it was any good; she hadn't heard of the writer before.

Captain Parfait, who had just been fed, climbed up into her lap and started purring, which meant that she couldn't get up. Who could disturb a purring cat? No one. That was why cats did it.

The chapters flew by. The book really wasn't bad. She was already mentally adding it to her order list to pick up for several of her customers. Captain Parfait had long since fallen asleep, making little kitty snores on her lap. Owning a bookstore was like owning her own private library.

She should really reread Lance Mitchell's book on French cinema. She had been so impressed with it before she had met its author. Would her opinion have changed? Sometimes that happened. A book that she had previously found enchanting would seem to fall flat upon a second reading. Or a book that she hadn't really cared for would come into focus, and she would find herself nodding at the author's sentences, agreeing with their outlook on the world.

Captain Parfait was still asleep on her lap, though, so she kept reading her novel. When she had finished it, she twisted around in the chair, looking for a slip of paper. Thank goodness the chair was so comfortable! She found the paper, wrote *5 copies* on it, and stuck it in the center of the book. She set it on the floor and moved on to the next book from the stack beside her on the table.

As she started reading, thoughts about Lance Mitchell's murder started to percolate in her mind.

Many people working on the movie set would have had a reason to kill him. Some of those people she hadn't even met yet. Trying to narrow down people by motive would be useless. Method? Cyanide wasn't something that would occur to your average, everyday murderer. The murder method, in most real-life murders, made the murderer obvious. There were men who shot their wives and children then tried to blame it on a burglar while keeping a straight face. There were murders staged to look like accidents even when the only people around were the ones who were most likely to profit. There were even murders committed from caretakers withholding medicine from someone who needed it to survive. Cyanide? Anymore, cyanide poisonings were accidental chemical exposures. There were so many tests that could prove the presence of cyanide that it really wasn't a good choice as a murder method. *Everyone* suspected it. So, who could possibly have used it?

Maybe she was thinking too hard. Who would inherit? That was a good question. Did Lance Mitchell have any kids?

She pulled the scrap of paper out of the book she'd just read and jotted *LM kids?* on it.

Should she do what Mickey suggested? Get a private detective license? Join a group of online sleuths? She wrote *online sleuths???* on the piece of paper. It might be a good idea. They might be able to give her some advice, like what *not* to do. She needed to keep her butt covered legally. Finding out how to do that would be nice.

Had Lance been accidentally poisoned? All alone in his room at the B&B? Probably not. She needed to find out whether he had been anywhere else before he'd gone to his room that night. Where could he have even run into cyanide? It wasn't like it was still being used as rat poison, was it? Was there an exterminator working on the set? She had never hired an exterminator. Were there exterminators on the island? Or did they have to come from the mainland?

She kept turning pages, not really following the story any longer.

Who would have had access to Lance Mitchell's room? No, that wasn't the important question. Who would have had access to the cupcakes, that was the question. Mickey, obviously. Had he delivered the cupcakes himself, or had someone else delivered them for him? Wait, didn't Jo say Lance purchased the cupcakes from the bakery? Or was the poisoned cupcake one of the cupcakes that Angie herself had brought to the set the day before? They would have been stale, but still.

Well, at least she could eliminate herself as a suspect, even if Detective Bailey wasn't able to. He had asked her a lot of questions but hadn't really let on to any theories about who had done it or when.

If the cupcake had been from the batch that she had taken with her from the bookstore, then the murderer could be anyone. Those cupcakes had been in the case for hours, and then they had been left out at the set. But how could someone be sure they would kill the right person that way? Or was the murderer some kind of psychopath who got off on randomly killing people?

She didn't think that was the case. There really weren't a lot of cases involving random poisonings. When *those* came up, it usually turned out to be a specific person that the murderer wanted to kill, and any other victims were simply collateral damage as the murderer tried to cover their trail.

The poisoned cupcake had to have come directly from the bakery. Lance Mitchell, she recalled, had gone to the bakery after he had left the coffee shop on Sunday morning. While there, he had complained about her coffee to Mickey, who had become so angry that he had stopped speaking for several hours. He must have bought cupcakes then.

Who else besides Mickey and Lance Mitchell would have had access to that batch of cupcakes?

The staff at the B&B, because they would have had a key to Lance's room.

And, presumably, Lance's assistant. It took Angie a moment to come up with his name, but soon she had jotted the name *Lloyd Rapinski* onto the scrap of paper. She had already spent time with Julia's assistant, Lucy Smith. Now to figure out how to catch up with Mr. Rapinski.

Surely Lloyd Rapinski, that clearly terrified, put-upon man, had a motive to kill his boss. He probably had several. Poisoners tended to be people who wanted to control the world, but who hated confrontation.

And Lloyd Rapinski obviously hated confrontation.

She might have just solved the mystery. That was the trick though, turning suspicion into proof.

Her cell phone rang. It was in her purse all the way on the other side of the stockroom. She sighed, then lifted Captain Parfait off her lap as carefully as she could, easing him back onto the cushion. She strode across the room and picked up the phone.

"Hello?"

She was answered by a sigh. "This is Detective Bailey, ma'am. I have some unpleasant news."

Angie looked around, found the folding chair in front of her inventory computer, and sat down. Her heart was racing. "I'm sitting down. What is it?"

"I've had to arrest the Jerritt twins."

"For what?" Angie asked incredulously. It couldn't be for the murder.

"For Lance Mitchell's murder, ma'am."

"Good grief, why?"

"The chief of police came under some heavy pressure to make an arrest, by some very important people on the island, because Hollywood exerted some heavy pressure on them. I can't name any names, but you get the picture."

"I do, detective," she said. Detective Bailey really shouldn't have told her any of this.

Detective Bailey continued, "I don't recommend coming to see them just yet. I'll send you a text when their mother leaves. She's been saying some unnecessary things about you over the last few minutes, and I'd stay away from her if you can."

"Thanks for the warning, detective. I'll wait for your text."

"Where are you?"

"At the bookstore."

"I might as well just send someone to pick you and your bicycle up."

"Oh, the bicycle's out at Jellicoe House! I completely forgot."

"Why would it be out there?" Detective Bailey asked suspiciously.

Angie sighed. "I don't *want* to turn into the crazy old cat lady detective of Nantucket Island, but apparently I don't have a choice. The cards are stacked against me." When the detective didn't respond, she added, "It's a long story."

He said, "I have a car out at Jellicoe House now, trying to keep peace between the movie folks and the press. I'll have them bring the bicycle back into town for you."

"Thank you," she said, shutting her eyes for a moment. Her head was spinning.

"See you soon."

~

A few minutes later, a squad car dropped her off at the police station, a large, new red brick building with white trim. Angie had barely had time to grab her purse and lock up the bookstore before the car had arrived.

She rushed inside and was quickly escorted to the jail cells, which had heavy, black, modern-looking doors. This wasn't the kind of old-fashioned prison where a prisoner could trick a guard out of their keys. The last time she'd been here, which was to visit Walter while he'd been arrested as a suspect in his father's murder, she had been shown into a private visitor's area. This time she was shown directly into an unlocked but not unguarded cell, where Mickey sat calmly on his bed and Jo paced around the room like a caged fox.

"This is so stupid," Jo said, looking up at Angie. "Oh, yeah, and you missed the part where Mom called you all kinds of nasty things for not having already solved the case. I told her if she said another word I was going to punch her in the mouth, so she called me a bunch of names and then left."

"That explains why they came for me so quickly," Angie said. She explained about the call from Detective Bailey.

"Why is this happening?" Jo demanded.

"Ultimately, because someone from Hollywood told the police to arrest someone, or else."

"Is this some kind of cover-up?"

"I doubt it," Angie said. "I don't think they had Lance assassinated like something out of *The Godfather* or anything."

"Then why arrest somebody now? It's only been a couple of days since the man died."

"Because there are too many suspects with motives, it's too weird of a way to die to just cover it up, and there's a bottleneck that implicates that the only people who had access to the cupcakes were you, Mickey, Lance Mitchell, and one other person."

"Who?"

"His assistant, Lloyd Rapinski. After I get done talking to you guys, I'm going to make sure that Detective Bailey checks him out."

Mickey stood up, holding his arms out. Angie gave him a hug.

"Go on," he said. "We don't need your company as much as we need to get out of jail. I have desserts to test for Sheldon's. I have pastries to make for you and half the island. I don't have time to play the Hollywood fall guy. Although, if I must say, I am handsome enough to do so."

Jo snorted.

Angie checked with Detective Bailey; he had indeed questioned Lloyd Rapinski about his whereabouts on Sunday afternoon and evening, as well as early Monday morning. For most of the time in question, Lloyd had been on his laptop in his room, using the B&B's Wi-Fi to make Internet calls. He was literally on camera the entire time. He did *not* have a key to Lance Mitchell's room; his room and possessions were searched. The keys for the room were the metal kind that had to be individually cut, not plastic key cards. None of the hardware stores that cut keys in town reported having cut keys for Mr. Rapinski or anyone else from the movie crew since they had arrived.

Angie went home. She didn't have the heart to tell Jo and Mickey that there was nothing she could do.

When she arrived at the cottage, the bicycle was already leaning against the side of the house. Aunt Margery was sitting in the living room, rereading an old Ngaio Marsh paperback.

"You went in to the bookstore," Aunt Margery said accusingly.

Angie's resolve not to tell her a word broke immediately. "Yes. But I didn't *do* anything. I went to pick up some new books and Captain

Parfait sat in my lap. So, you see, I had to stay. And then Detective Bailey called me about Jo and Mickey."

Aunt Margery sighed.

Angie said, "I thought of the assistant maybe having a key to Lance's room, but he didn't, and he was making internet calls all night, so he has a fairly decent alibi." She sat down in an armchair next to her great-aunt. "Aunt Margery, I'm in over my head. I can't do this. I'm just going to let the police handle it. They don't really think Jo or Mickey did anything. It's just a political move to keep Hollywood happy. They'll be out of jail soon."

"Do you have any other leads?" Aunt Margery asked.

"If I do, my mind has completely blanked out about them."

Aunt Margery closed her book around her finger. "My advice to you, Miss Agatha Mary Clarissa Christie Prouty, is to let yourself relax as much as possible. Something will come to you. If not a solution, then the next step that you need to come to a solution."

"I haven't found out anything yet," Angie said. "It's a little early to be talking about solutions."

"You have found out that Lloyd Rapinski had an alibi for Sunday and Monday. Eliminate the impossible, you know."

*...whatever remains, no matter how improbable, must be the truth.*

"I know, I know," Angie said, "but that's what Sherlock Holmes says, and I'm only Angie the Watson."

"Then make the most reasonable guess you can and try to force the person to confess," Aunt Margery said. "Who knows? That might even work."

"I hate that," Angie said. "I'd rather have the incontrovertible proof *and* the confession."

"Me, too," Aunt Margery said.

Angie sighed. "I'll be at the store. I'm giving up on the whole day off concept. And I think I want to reread Lance Mitchell's book."

# Chapter 10

# BACKGROUND RESEARCH

Angie started her research by taking care of the items on her scrap of paper. She ordered five more copies of the first novel she had been reading. Then she looked up Lance's biography online and discovered that he had never been married and had never had children.

She did a few searches for online amateur mystery groups but hesitated at actually signing up for one of them. She had been in several online groups over the years. There were good groups and bad ones, and all of them had their own peculiarities, rules that made no sense, and in-group politics. Probably amateur sleuth groups were no different. She should sign up for a group or two, but *after* this case was done, so she could devote some time to feeling them out when she wasn't in the middle of a case.

The phone listings for the island included two different exterminators. She called the first one and found out that they didn't use cyanide in any of their poisons. It just had too bad of a reputation, and none of the clients wanted it around. At the second one, the owner's wife recognized her name and said, "So do you need an exterminator for the bookstore...or is this about the Lance Mitchell case?"

Angie came clean, saying that she wasn't officially investigating the case, but she was bothered by some of the details that were coming out in rumors.

"Mmm-hmm," said the owner's wife. "Well, we don't use cyanide for any of our exterminations. We just don't operate on that scale. Some of the chemicals we use are more dangerous, though. From what I heard, the presence of cyanide hasn't been confirmed. I wouldn't rule out some type of rat poison, but it might be some other chemical doing the same kind of damage."

Angie had the woman list the names of the chemicals that they were using, but when she researched them, they didn't seem to cause the same symptoms: none of them seemed to work by cutting off the oxygen supply and making the victim actually choke. There was also that detail about the horrible red rash they found on Lance.

She researched Lance's book and discovered that it had also been made into a documentary, which in fact had given Lance his big break. The book hadn't been famous until it had been turned into film. She made a note to watch the documentary later.

The next logical step would be to bicycle to Jellicoe House and question the staff to find out Lance's movements that night, as well as find out who had been in his room.

She didn't seriously suspect them just because they'd had access to Lance's room. They had the opportunity to tamper with one of the cupcakes, however, they didn't have any motive. Dealing with entitled tourists was their business, and Lance would be just one more jerk as far as they were concerned.

The woman at the front desk of Jellicoe House was a beautiful, dark-haired, middle-aged woman with a nametag labeled Mariam S. Angie recognized her, but they hadn't really spoken before.

After a few moments of polite small talk, Angie inquired if she could ask her a few questions about Lance Mitchell.

"He was demanding, but we've had worse. I made sure none of the teenagers who clean rooms for us came anywhere near him. Either I or Mrs. Keene, one of the owners, did his room and handled his calls. Standard procedure."

"Just checking," Angie said.

"What are you, a private detective?"

"No, just a busybody who happens to be Mickey and Jo Jerritt's best friend."

Mariam's shoulders relaxed a little. "In that case, I can understand being curious!"

"I own the bookstore in town. Pastries and Page-Turners."

"Oh!" the woman said. "I've been meaning to get out there, but I'm so busy. Is there any chance that you could arrange for us to get some gently used bestsellers out here? Easy beach reads, basically?"

Angie quickly arranged to bring a stack of books over to the B&B on the following day. Mariam said she would see if any of the current guests wanted anything specific.

"Can you tell me," Angie said after the book business was wrapped up, "what happened on Saturday and Sunday? Who cleaned the room, what time Mr. Mitchell came and left, and whether—I know this is less than professional, but it would clear Mickey and Jo, and that's all I really care about—anyone, um, stole a cupcake and ate it or anything?"

Mariam laughed. "Well, I was the one who cleaned his room on Saturday. He must have had someone spend the night on Friday because there was makeup smeared on the bathroom mirror," Angie's eyes widened. "Anyways, nobody else from staff went into the room. The girls avoided it like the plague, you can be sure, and Mrs. Keene and I didn't get a call for anything else from him that day."

"Did anyone eat any cupcakes?" Angie asked hopefully.

"I didn't. Tempting, but I'm on a low-carb diet." She tilted her head, staring into space. "Let me think about the guests coming and going...of course you can't keep an eye on them all the time, like I told Detective Bailey."

"Of course," Angie agreed.

"Mr. Mitchell left his room at seven a.m. on Sunday morning. An early riser for someone in the film industry. I started cleaning his room a few minutes after he left, just to be sure that I wouldn't have to run into him any more than necessary. Everyone else was up by ten a.m., with Miss Julia being the latest riser. Ms. Smith, her assistant, had risen much earlier, about five in the morning, and left for a run along the beach and the trails, returning around six or six-ten. The others came down, had breakfast, and left. I'm assuming you don't want to know about anyone else staying at the B&B other than the people working on the film?"

"I might later, but not for now."

"One of the actors came back at about ten a.m., went into his room, and then left again straightaway. Other than that, no one returned until two in the afternoon, when Mr. Mitchell and his assistant, and Miss Julia and her assistant, Ms. Smith, all returned together."

"How did they seem?"

"A bit chilly toward each other, I think. None of them were saying much."

"Did they have the cupcakes?"

"I don't know for sure, but Mr. Mitchell's assistant had a flat white box. It had this big ribbon tied to the top – hot pink and bright green. Couldn't miss it."

Angie nodded. Mickey and Jo put those ribbons on the bakery boxes that they sold directly to customers. They tended to skip putting ribbons on any boxes that Angie used at the bookstore, though, and the box that she had left on the set on Saturday definitely didn't have one. That meant that the box they were carrying was the box from Sunday.

"I can't be sure, but I think so," Mariam said. "I didn't see them go into the rooms, but the assistant immediately came downstairs and left again, to where I don't know. Probably to the set."

"But you're not sure."

Mariam shook her head. "Julia, her assistant, and the woman with all the tattoos left about three. Then there was nothing until a large group of people arrived at nine; they were very loud, Mrs. Keene had to go upstairs to make sure that they quieted down and didn't disturb the other guests."

"Who was in the large group? Was it just the people who had rooms here?"

Again Mariam shook her head. "I don't know all their names. There were people I recognized but that didn't actually have rooms. Later, several people left...about ten forty-five? It was just after I'd gone to bed for the night, but before I had really fallen asleep. I try to keep an ear open in case one of the guests needs something."

Angie thought about what Mariam had said. "Wait. Didn't Mr. Mitchell leave to go to supper? Or have it delivered?"

"If he did, I didn't see it," Mariam said. "I thought it was strange, too. But then maybe he just ate cupcakes all night. Some people would, especially if they had a sweet tooth. He called to have tea brought up at about eleven, Earl Gray. Which he complained about. I saw a pair of white boxes on the desk in his room when I delivered the tea."

"Did you see the one with the ribbon?"

"Yes, there was a pink and green ribbon on the top box at least."

Angie thanked Mariam, saying that she wasn't sure what to look into next, but that she still had hopes of getting Mickey and Jo out from behind bars.

The fact was, she expected them to be released at any time, whether she did anything or not.

"Detective Bailey," she said as she leaned her bike against a nearby tree. "I'm glad you stopped. I wanted to ask you something."

It almost seemed as though Detective Bailey had been looking for her. He had been driving slowly along Old South Road in his patrol car and had slowed down even further, pulling off the road almost as soon as she came into view, waiting for her to reach him.

"And I, you," he said.

"First, was cyanide used to kill Mr. Mitchell? The rash found on him is consistent with that kind of poison." she said.

"Looks like you've done your research. We don't have official results back on that yet," Detective Bailey said with a sigh. "But my assessment agrees with yours. Lance Mitchell sure seemed to have been poisoned, and cyanide seems plausible."

She nodded. "Second, are there any results on what the contents of Mr. Mitchell's stomach were? I'm assuming there were signs of cupcake in there, or you wouldn't have arrested Jo and Mickey. But was there anything else?"

Detective Bailey shook his head. "The medical examiner arrived already and did the autopsy pronto. Fastest response from Boston I've ever seen. But as far as she could tell, there was nothing in there but cupcake."

"Any chance that the medical examiner could tell what type of cupcake?"

"That went in for analysis. I asked that question, too, and the answer was that Mr. Mitchell was a good chewer, so she couldn't be sure."

Angie blinked. "A what?"

"Some people," Detective Bailey said, "apparently don't chew their food really well, and it's easier to do a physical analysis on what they ate before they died. Or so the medical examiner says. But Mr. Mitchell chewed well, and the material in his stomach was an undistinguished mush."

"Okay," Angie said.

"Anything else?"

"One more thing, so far. Why are you being so cooperative? Normally you tell me to keep my distance."

Detective Bailey made a face. "I should probably tell you to keep your nose out of this one, too. But I just have a feeling about this. I'm going to find out who did the deed, and then I'm going to be told that I found out no such thing, thank you very much, Hollywood will take care of Hollywood all by itself. And then the murderer will just fade out of view. If a civilian comes up with the murderer, and then makes that information public...well, wouldn't that just be too bad?"

"You're using me?"

"You might say I'm returning the favor, little miss I-wanted-to-ask-you-something."

"That's fair," she agreed. "So, let's call it a temporary truce for the moment. What did you want to ask me?"

"Get anywhere?"

"I don't seem to have narrowed down the list of suspects whatsoever," she said. "Sorry."

He shrugged. "Maybe we can help each other out. I can review your suspect list – I don't think there's any police protocol stopping me."

All the strength in her arms seemed to flow out her feet. Her shoulders slumped, and her hands dropped to her sides. "Wait – you know who did it already?"

Bailey laughed. Then he gave her a stern look. "Do you really think I'm the kind of man who would let a murderer walk free a minute longer than I had to?"

"When you put it like that," she said, "not really."

"That's right. If I need you to accidentally spill the beans after I solve the case, I'll pull you in. Unofficially, of course. Have you made any other progress?"

She told him about her research online, then about her discussion with Mariam. "And, since I found out that Mr. Mitchell hadn't eaten anything else that night, I think the next thing to do is talk to Jeanette."

"Jeanette?"

She explained that Jeanette had known Mr. Mitchell back in the day, in France, and that she had talked to her earlier about Lance Mitchell.

"I want to see if I can get anything else out of her, now that Julia Withers and Lucy Smith aren't around," she concluded.

"And you didn't think to mention that earlier?" he asked.

"I don't know what you don't know," she said. "Also...there's so much happening that it's hard to keep track of it all. Maybe I should start carrying around a notebook."

Detective Bailey exhaled slowly. "I thank you for your time." Then he seemed to perk up, almost sniffing the breeze. "If you'll excuse me..."

He drove about a hundred feet down the road, then parked off the shoulder behind a particularly thick cluster of trees.

One of the VW Microbuses that the film crew was using for transportation came into view, clearly speeding. It whooshed by Angie, making her bike shudder a little as it passed.

Detective Bailey's patrol car lit up and went into motion. It was like watching a nature show, the kind where the gazelle doesn't survive to the end of the episode. Soon the Microbus was pulled over to the side of the road and Detective Bailey was writing up a ticket.

Angie pedaled back toward town, which forced her to pass the Microbus. She couldn't help but notice that Sandra Potvin and some of the other crew members were inside, looking bored and annoyed. They spotted Angie almost immediately and waved her down.

"Hey, bookstore lady!" someone called, it was the blond man who had the black eye, the Yankees fan. He looked so familiar still.

She stopped. "Yes?"

Where had she seen him before meeting him at the bookstore? She just couldn't remember.

"We're having a bonfire on the beach tonight. Want to come? You seem okay."

It would be a good opportunity to interview suspects. "Sure. Where?"

"Uh..."

Sandra Potvin pushed the blond guy out of the window. "Nobadeer Beach," she said, rolling her eyes. "We'll be there by sunset at least, and onward, if it doesn't storm. Bring a bottle of vodka and these idiots will love you forever."

The rest of the crew cheered, causing Detective Bailey to give them a dirty look.

"I'll try to make it," Angie said, laughing.

Her stomach growled as she rode up to Sheldon's Shuckery. If she didn't watch it, she was going to get fat from eating there so often. She shook her head. Not today: her willpower was strong.

Five minutes later, Jeanette brought her a huge plate of a little something and Angie was laughing at herself: so much for willpower. Whatever the dish was, it had Creole ancestry and seemed to involve a lot of cream, some crayfish, and trout fried in cornmeal and almonds.

It was delicious. Jeanette sat next to her at the table in the main dining room, drinking a cup of coffee and picking at a bread roll. "What I knew about Lance Mitchell..." she said. "I told you everything I know for certain."

"I'm getting stuck," Angie said. "I need to know what you suspect."

"What I suspect? I suspect many things." The way Jeanette was sitting with one hand under her chin, two fingers along her cheek, made Angie think she was holding an invisible cigarette. "You're right. There is something that I didn't want to say in front of the others. You know that the actress, Mademoiselle Julia, was his lover at the time he wrote the book?"

"I knew they were together at some point," Angie said, "but I wasn't sure of the timing."

"They met each other then. The fights they would get into! Whenever they were together, the sparks would fly. But they should not have stayed together. I think that Mademoiselle Julia should have fled from him! He was always so cold and cruel. And she would say, 'Oh, it is only his manner in public, he is so tender in private.'"

"But he wasn't?"

Jeanette shrugged. "A man who cannot honor his woman in public is lying in private. But she would say that she could change him, that she could save him from himself. Truly though, I think she was trying to save herself."

"Save herself from what?"

"Youth? Innocence? Naïveté? Not having a grand passion to keep her warm at night?" Jeanette snorted, rolling up the bread between her fingers. "Other women wanted the man; therefore, he must have some worth. I think that was the answer. We were all a little in desire of him, not to keep forever, but to possess him for a night or two."

"Did...you...?" Angie asked.

"A lady never tells," Jeanette said, looking so serious for a moment that Angie had to wonder: had she slept with Lance Mitchell? Then Jeanette smiled. "No, no, by the time I knew Lance I had already met my Sheldon. Monsieur Mitchell was no temptation for me." But her face looked closed and restrained suddenly, as if there were something about the situation that she didn't want to bring up.

"Was there anyone else who was especially jealous?"

"Oh, only about a dozen different women." She leaned closer to Angie. "But there *is* something I can tell you that I think you don't know, now that I think of it. It has nothing to do with his women, either! It is about the book."

"What about it?" Angie asked.

"When he first started writing it, he was writing it with someone else!"

"How do you know that?"

"Well, he was very mysterious about it. He refused to say what he was working on at all, but he would talk about the work. 'Today our progress has been very poor.' 'Today we are making great strides in discovering the methods that so-and-so uses to edit his films!' Things like that. He would let slip that "we" more often than he should have, and then when the book was published, the mysterious *we* became the singular *I*."

"So, his cowriter never got credit...or they fell out early in the process?"

Jeanette shook her head. "I do not think that it was so soon. That 'we' continued almost all the way to the end. He was all happiness until his book was accepted, and then he took on a darker, angrier mood. Others said that it was the publication of his book that changed him, but I disagree. From the way he fought with Mademoiselle Julia, I can only think that his temper has always been the same. But after the book was published, his temper became worse."

"I think I understand," Julia said. "He screwed someone else out of the book credit, but he never got over feeling guilty about it. Do you think he did most of the writing? Or did his partner do that?"

"I think he did most of the writing," Jeanette said. "I had heard him speak enough that I recognize his voice in the writing, both in the English and the French versions."

"There are two?"

"Yes, both versions came out at the same time. The book is known well in America, but it is quite famous in France. He spoke French well, but with an accent. It was like listening to a mafioso speak French."

"Maybe that was why all the women wanted him," Angie joked.

Jeanette seemed to take her seriously. "It was part of his charm, to be sure."

"Who do you think the other writer was?"

"I don't know," she said, her voice stiff again. Her eyes roamed around the dining room, fastening on Sheldon as he came out from the kitchen, bearing an armload of plates and a wide grin.

He made a kissing face at her as he passed. She smiled back, then looked down at the bread roll, which she had completely destroyed. Before Angie could ask anything else, she stood up, gesturing toward Angie's plate, which she had picked almost completely clean. "I think the dish is a success, yes?"

Angie nodded her head up and down, shoving in the last bite.

Sheldon returned to squeeze Jeanette around the waist. "So, has our resident sleuth gotten my bakers out of jail yet? I can't wow everyone this summer without a spectacular new dessert!"

Angie shook her head. "At least Jeanette seems to have the new dish worked out, whatever it is."

"You like it?"

She started praising Jeanette's cooking, but Sheldon held out his hand. "Stop, stop, I already know how wonderful she is, you don't need to tell me. You need to tell your customers at the bookstore!"

She promised she would. Sheldon brought her a bill that was far lower than the lunch was worth. She walked back to the bookstore, wheeling the bicycle alongside her. She didn't trust herself not to lurch around like a water balloon on stilts if she tried to ride it.

Had it been Sheldon who had helped write the book? He had started out as a screenwriter, after all.

If he had gotten screwed over by Lance, it might explain why he had suddenly decided to go back to the U.S. and start a restaurant.

And why Jeanette had seemed so secretive all the sudden.

Chapter 11

# A HOT, BRIGHT FLAME

Returning to her hideout at the bookstore, Angie tucked herself back in her comfy chair and started rereading Lance Mitchell's book. At first, she forced herself to slow down and take notes. Her memory was good enough for most books, but was it good enough for a murder case?

She quickly got buried in trying to write down every single detail, no matter how insignificant. Everything seemed significant. Nothing stood out as an actual clue, though.

She put the notebook aside and went back to her normal reading method. She had always read at her own pace: very, very quickly. Her parents and teachers had always tried to tell her to slow down; they clearly thought she couldn't understand what she was reading because she was turning the pages so fast! But, unless the book was just flat-out poorly written, it always seemed that the information presented in the book felt more natural to her—as though she had always known it—when she read at her normal speed.

Aunt Margery, who didn't read as fast as Angie did, had been the only one to understand.

Angie read the entire book from front to back, the same way she had before, found nothing, and started to put it down—then caught herself. She hadn't read the endnotes last time, and she had almost passed them by again.

She read them. Unfortunately, reading them out of context, they didn't make sense. She was going to have to read the book *again*, this time flipping back and forth between text and endnotes to get them all sorted out. What a pain. At least it was a good book.

The phone rang. Once again, it was all the way across the room in her purse. She should just ignore it. At least this time, Captain Parfait hadn't been sitting on her lap.

Walking over to the phone, Angie glanced down and saw the word "Walter" flash across her screen. No. No way. She was *not* getting pulled into a phone call with him.

Angie nervously paced around the room until her phone stopped ringing. Almost immediately after it stopped, a text message alert dinged. Curious, she grabbed her phone with shaking hands. What did he have to say? Did he want to get back together?

"Hey Angie. It's Walter. Just checking in to see how everything is going "

That nosy jerk. Of course he didn't want to get back together. He clearly just wanted to know how the case was going.

Angie snatched her phone up and fired off a brief response: "Fine. Thanks."

There was a quick text back from Walter: "Great. Happy to hear it. How is the case with Lance Mitchell going?"

She rolled her eyes up towards the ceiling. Yep, there it was - the only information Walter was after. He probably just wanted this swept under the rug to appease the other powerful, rich people governing the island.

"Not solved. Don't know who did it. Is that it, Walter?" Their breakup still stung. After all, it had only been two months since Walter dumped her. She hadn't heard from him a single time since that horrible night out on the beach! Angie couldn't help but feel angry at Walter for being forced to discuss the case. She thought she was being taken for granted, both by Walter and by the entire island.

"Yes, sorry to bug you. Hope Jo and Mickey are doing okay."

Oh, the nerve of that man, bringing Jo and Mickey up. He had to know that was a sore spot for her. Angie threw her phone back into her purse and felt her body shudder. She hoped she never saw Walter's face again.

Back to business. There were more important things to worry about than texts from an ex-boyfriend.

Angie's next pass through Lance Mitchell's book proved to be about as useful as the previous two. She flipped back and forth through the endnotes, tracking down which one went where. It was frustrating. There was something in the book that was relevant to the murder, or at least to the identity of Lance's co-writer, but she couldn't put a finger on it. An incongruity of some kind.

She riffled through the pages, letting her fingers stop wherever they wanted. They stopped on a page early on in the book that mentioned some of the lost films of famed early director Georges Méliès, who, in frustration, had burned all the film negatives he had on hand after he lost his film studio. The event was considered one of the great tragedies of film history.

The main text of the book read, "It must have been really something to see the burning of all that film. Film—which is made of cellulose nitrate, or celluloid—burns fast and with a hot, bright flame. Not only that, but it puts out copious quantities of poisonous gas. It is one of the great ironies of film that showing it means bringing it closer to ruin. This is also, undoubtedly, a part of the thrill of film. What creates the magic of film in small amounts—the light and heat of the projector—can, in larger amounts, cause both the destruction of the film and the death of its patrons."

An endnote at the bottom of the paragraph led her to a note at the back of the book. She could remember it almost word for word, but turned to the note just to be certain:

"Once it begins burning, celluloid film requires no oxygen for the flames to continue, even to spread. That's why falsely shouting *fire* in a crowded theater has such a negative connotation. To shout *fire* in a crowded theater is like announcing that a bomb is about to go off, as all the negatives in the theater begin to burn. At least, that's how my father, a noted chemist, explained it to me as a child."

The two passages didn't quite resemble each other in tone, not exactly. For one thing, the first passage seemed almost gleeful about the possibility of film burning; the second one seemed as if it were written by someone who wasn't quite such a pyromaniac.

Angie dropped into the chair in front of her inventory computer and jumped over to the Internet. She looked up Lance Mitchell on Wikipedia and discovered that his father had been a warehouse attendant in New Jersey and his mother had been a schoolteacher.

Bingo. She'd found her first clue - at least, her first clue to the identity of the second writer. Or at least that there *was* one. One who happened to have a chemist for a father.

Who was it, though?

It could be anyone. She sighed. All the research she was doing seemed completely useless. Mickey and Jo were still in jail. She was wasting her time.

At least, that's what her head was telling her.

Her gut was telling her something else. It was saying that perhaps the co-writer hadn't just quietly slipped into the background, allowing Lance Mitchell to steal the glory for *their* book. Exactly how far would a scorned co-writer go to enact revenge?

"Any luck?" Aunt Margery asked, looking up from her spot in the living room recliner where she was just finishing up the Ngaio Marsh novel she'd started reading earlier.

"Walter texted me," Angie said with a grimace.

"And how is *he*?" Aunt Margery asked.

"He's just like everyone else, wanting to know when I'll have the case solved."

"At which point you bit his head off, I suppose," Aunt Margery said.

"Eh. I didn't go *that* far."

"It's after lunch. Have you eaten?"

Angie said, "I'm fine. I treated myself to Sheldon's."

"Ah," Aunt Margery said. Leaning back in her chair and closing her eyes, she said, "Jeanette's French."

It wasn't that Angie didn't want to tell Aunt Margery all about what she'd learned from Jeanette. It just felt like Angie's subconscious was trying to protect her from saying something out loud that she wasn't quite sure of. The hint in her subconscious that had taken her to the endnote in Lance Mitchell's book was trying to lead her somewhere else, and if she thought about it too hard, she would end up destroying the tiny little niggling hint.

It would be better to just go at her own pace, she decided. Let it come to her naturally instead of trying to force it for Aunt Margery's sake.

So instead of telling Aunt Margery about the sort-of-clues that she'd been trying to track down, she told her about the dish that Jeanette had made for her and asked if Jeanette had been a smoker back in the day.

"When she arrived here from France, she quit after about a month," Aunt Margery said. "She said that if she couldn't have the French brand that she liked, she would rather have none at all. I understand she smokes like a coal train when she goes back to visit family. Then she quits all over again when she comes back to the States."

Angie laughed. "She has more willpower than most people."

"She's very strong," Aunt Margery agreed.

"She told me the story about how she and Sheldon met," Angie said. "At least, she told me more of the story than I've heard before."

"True love," Aunt Margery said. "Did she tell you about the part where he stole her practically out from underneath her lover at the time, the film director?"

"She hinted at it," Angie admitted.

"You wouldn't think it, to look at Sheldon," Aunt Margery said. "He's never been what you could call handsome! But the French think of their men differently than we do, or at least they did. Men we would consider ugly, French women often think of as virile. It's all about that certain look in the eye, that purely masculine mischief. It cannot be hidden."

"Sheldon usually looks mischievous," Angie agreed. "Plus, he must have been an excellent cook, even back then. That's got to be important, if you're French."

"She's the better cook of the two of them," Aunt Margery said, winking at her.

"What's so special about him, then? What made her leave her lover for him?"

"He wrote her poetry," Aunt Margery said.

"What? He's a poet?" Angie laughed. "I never would have guessed."

"It was terrible poetry," Aunt Margery said. "The worst. Very clever... very funny...utterly filthy!"

They both laughed.

"Okay, that I can imagine," Angie said. "At any rate, he wants Mickey and Jo out of jail so they can develop a showstopper dessert for him for this summer, something that all the tourists will want. Something that will get him onto the lifestyle pages in the Boston pages, I'd imagine."

"I've heard that Mickey is a bit bored of making cupcakes."

"I've heard that, too," Angie said.

"What are your plans for this evening?"

"The good news is that I won't need to eat for another year at least," Angie said, patting her stomach. "I've been invited to a beach party on Nobadeer Beach with the film crew. I'm supposed to bring a bottle of vodka and hope the cops don't bust us—it'll be just like high school."

"You didn't go to too many parties in high school if I recall correctly."

"Oh, Mickey and Jo and I got in enough trouble as it was, if I recall *correctly*," Angie laughed to herself. Jo had settled down quite a bit over the years, but she could still be more than a handful. Too bad she was still stuck in jail; she could easily get everyone at the party talking about what Angie wanted to know.

Like what their parents did for a living.

Angie arrived at Nobadeer Beach at nine o'clock with a bottle of vodka, a big jug of orange juice, and red plastic cups. If the film crew was going to go with a high school beach party theme, then she was going to go all the way with her contribution, too.

Nobadeer Beach was becoming somewhat infamous as *the* place to party on the Fourth of July. Thousands of people would show up. As a local who sold books, she avoided the place like the plague. The traffic was a headache and the noise from all the fireworks was even worse. The morning after, the entire beach would be trashed. The police had worked hard last year to keep the insanity down to a manageable level, cracking down on underage drinking, fistfights, trespassing, and littering—glass bottles shattered on public beaches was no joke. Little kids played there.

But that night the beach was almost empty, except for the film crew.

The night was beautiful, a clear sky with a full moon. The breeze blew in from the ocean, but it wasn't so strong that it kicked up the sand. Dozens of camp chairs were scattered around a huge bonfire. A pit for a clambake had been set up and was steaming with a mouth-watering aroma but it had yet to be opened up. Nobody was supposed to light a bonfire on a public beach, let alone hold a clambake, but obviously the rules were being bent tonight. Not a single cop was in sight.

*Hollywood is like high school, except with fewer cops*, Angie decided.

She wasn't the only local to be invited, but most of the crowd belonged to the film crew. Mariam was out on the beach, serving as a bartender at a bar made of plastic folding tables under a tent. Angie was surprised to see the setup; she wondered if the B&B had organized the party for the crew.

Several people were playing guitars next to the fire, trying to work their way through the dueling banjo scene from *Deliverance,* and failing. Angie suspected that show tunes would be played soon. At least one of them had to have been in a production of *Man of La Mancha*.

She walked up to the bar, handed Mariam the vodka and orange juice and cups, and said, "Um. This is a bigger deal than I thought it would be."

"Don't worry, love," Mariam said, taking the offerings. "We're not getting arrested tonight."

"This feels more like a celebration than a wake," Angie said.

"Doesn't it? I wonder why." Mariam winked and handed Angie back a screwdriver in one of her red plastic cups, with ice and a slice of orange in it. Angie took it and sipped, then gave Mariam a thumb's up.

Several of the crew who had been in the habit of hanging out at the bookstore for coffee greeted her, and she eventually found herself near the bonfire in a folding chair between Sandra Potvin and Al Petrillo, who had been her two favorites at the bookstore anyway.

Al Petrillo talked to her about books; Sandra Potvin talked to her about running a bookstore. It was almost like being brought in for official questioning, she was so thorough. She wanted to know everything from how Angie picked out which books to order, to where she got her coffee bean supply from.

"Planning to take over the bookstore?" Angie asked. "Lord knows I'm not competent enough to make a cup of coffee." She wasn't drunk, not exactly, but she was also on her third screwdriver.

Al had the kindness to deny that Angie needed to make a single change, but Sandra hesitated, staring into the flames.

"I've always been curious," she said finally. "When I was younger, I would become obsessed with something for six months or a year and learn everything I could about it. Then, when I ran out of books to read on the subject, I would bug my mother to take me somewhere that I could observe it. Grown-ups will teach you about anything if you're a kid and you're interested, and you're polite."

"Like what?"

"Makeup, for one thing," Sandra said. "I got stuck waiting around on sets for a while when I was thirteen or so, and I started following one of the makeup artists around. It was a disaster movie, so I learned a lot—not just how to make someone look more attractive or look a certain age, but how wounds should look like, too. Of course, the first thing I did was make it look like someone had given me a black eye. Mom panicked."

Angie chuckled. "And of course, it became your career, so you must have really loved it."

"Not especially," Sandra said, her jaw set firmly. "I thought I would be doing something else with my life, but it didn't turn out. Makeup was the backup plan that I never thought I would need."

"What was your original plan?" Angie asked.

"I was going to be a famous film director," Sandra said. "Even in a male-dominated industry, I was going to be so brilliant that of course I would be a success."

"Ahhh," said Al Petrillo. "*I* was going to be a famous crime writer. Although I did want to be a famous crime director too, but strictly as a fallback career."

"Oh?" Angie said.

"I have a good eye," he said, "otherwise I wouldn't have made it as a camera operator. I found, however, that I don't really have a sense of how to put together a plot. All the books I've read, you'd think it would come naturally to me by now. But no. I'd come up with all these great ideas and have no idea how to string events together to set up the cool parts." He chuckled. "I tried becoming a world-famous director, too, but Lance Mitchell soon made me realize the error of my ambitions."

"Oh, no!" Angie said. "What did he do?"

"Picked a project to pieces in front of me and about five of the most influential money men in the business. At least he had something nice to say about the actual camera work."

"What did you do?"

"I smiled and nodded until he was done, then all the money men had asked me whether I had any projects coming up as a cameraman. I got their business cards, thanked them, and fled. And I've been some form of camera operator ever since. A successful one. But I never directed anything again. The thought turns my stomach."

He gave her a grin to show that he was over it.

"I think that's rotten," Angie said. "That he said that to you, in public, in a way that—"

Al said, "It's all right. He's gone now. It's over."

Changing the subject, Angie asked Sandra, "What else have you obsessed over?"

She had pulled a wadded up, white paper bag out of her pocket, and tossed it into the flames. For a moment, all three of them watched the paper start to burn, even brighter than the surrounding flames. Then the piece of trash slipped between two branches and disappeared.

Sandra shook her head. "Let me think...films, of course...dinosaurs when I was a little kid, but I think most little kids do that...I used to design houses out of graham crackers and once made a Frank Lloyd Wright house, Fallingwater...I learned how to skateboard well enough to win a couple of youth tournaments...cooking...how to become a pirate...robotics...all things French...first aid...all things horses...Alice in Wonderland...mind reading...taxonomy...I'm a class A chess player, or at least I was before I got bored with it...Oh, and I can do a killer impression."

Angie smiled and said, "Please. I need to see proof of this."

Sandra took a big swill of the screwdriver in her hand and adjusted her posture, squaring her shoulders aggressively. "Yeah, I'm Lucy Smith. I work for *the* Julia Withers," Sandra barked, "I'll need a latte. Skim. You got that? *Skim* milk. Anything else does *not* follow Julia's diet and that is a *big* no-no."

Angie practically fell to the sand with laughter. Sandra was right – she really could do a great impression. It's like she had transformed – physically, vocally, everything – into Lucy right before Angie's eyes.

"So, what led a chess-playing, skateboarding girl to the world of makeup? After that impression, seems like you'd be a pretty good actress," Angie asked.

"A random string of events, that's what. But, you know, makeup was always interesting to me. Seeing how all those ingredients come together to make something beautiful... It's scientific in a way," Sandra had a distant look in her eye. She broke off. "Anyway, all this is to say that I've been thinking about getting out of the film industry, and you're in a talkative mood, *and* you're running a successful bookstore. So, I decided to pick your brains. I hope you don't mind."

"Not at all. Ask away."

More questions ensued, and Sandra asked, "Would you say that your success depends on pairing with the Nantucket Bakery or not?"

"I wouldn't say that the store's viability depends on the specific bakery," Angie said. "For the most part, I could totally get away with buying grocery store baked goods to sell to the tourists. I think my success is coming from a general policy of taking the long view, not the short one. A grocery store is never going to be loyal to me, but Jo and Mickey will always be loyal to me. Small businesses need to have each other's backs. They promote each other and build each other up. Or at least they should."

"What happens if they don't?"

Angie explained Nonatum's, the restaurant that had so snidely insulted Sheldon's Shuckery in the newspaper, and about how the locals were turning their noses up at the place in retaliation.

Sandra's face took on a satisfied look. "What goes around comes around, is that it?"

"Kind of. I think if you make other people's lives better, they will try to arrange it so that you can keep doing so. If you want to be cynical about it."

"And vice versa."

"Sure."

Al said, "You should write a book about how on a dark February night, a group of locals dance around this other restaurant as it burns, and the fire department looks on."

Angie and Sandra both turned toward him in surprise. Sandra said, "Al, I thought you were exaggerating about not being able to come up with serious plots. You weren't."

He belly-laughed. "If I had to plot out the story of who killed Lance Mitchell, I would make it so that an alien dressed up as a bear did it."

"There are no bears on Nantucket," Angie said.

"*There will be*," Al said in a mysterious, over-dramatic voice. They all laughed again.

Angie stared at the fire for a few moments, letting the flames drag her attention away. She seemed to see a face dancing in the flames. It flickered, then turned into Lance Mitchell's arrogant face. After a moment it became Julia Withers' face, crying, then going stiff and professional. Finally, the face became Lucy Smith's lips pressed tightly together.

"Who would you pick," Angie asked Sandra, "as the murderer?"

Sandra held a bottle of beer in one hand. She took a sip. "I would go the multiple-killer route, myself. Everyone hated him? Well, let's have *everyone* murder him. Agatha Christie did it. Why can't we?"

"I could see that if there were multiple stab wounds," Angie said. "But cyanide?"

Sandra turned her head slowly toward her. "He was killed by *cyanide*?"

"That's what they think so far," Angie said with a shrug.

"Isn't that a little old-fashioned? I mean, it's stupid easy to trace. Forensic researchers can track the chemicals at the drop of a hat."

Angie raised one eyebrow at Sandra.

"I think the police still have to figure out who gave him the poison and how," Angie responded.

Sandra snorted. "Probably one of those cupcakes. He was going nuts over them on the set. I thought he was going to stuff them all down his throat right there and then. Nobody else would touch them, they were so scared of getting yelled at. I heard he had every single one of them boxed up to take with him."

"Yep," Angie said. "I mean, that's what I heard, too. He was even trying to convince Mickey to move the bakery out to Los Angeles."

"And?"

"Mickey turned him down."

"It would be just like him to get himself poisoned, in a way, to spite someone who had turned him down," Sandra said.

"Wow."

"Yeah."

The pair of look-a-likes that Angie had seen at the Chamber of Commerce—the Yankee fan and the Detroit Tigers fan—crossed in front of them to claim a pair of folding chairs nearby. They pulled the chairs up next to Sandra.

"Hey, Sandra," said the Yankees fan. "How's it going?"

He and the Detroit Tigers fan *still* looked so familiar. "Jeez," Angie said, "I'm sorry. But who *are* you guys? We didn't get to have a formal introduction."

They both laughed heartily, sounding eerily similar.

"Oh, man," the Yankees fan said. "She doesn't know who you are, Rob."

The relatively attractive blond guy in the Detroit Tigers cap grinned and his face lit up. It transformed his face. *It was Rob Blake.* Her face turned hot, even the side facing away from the fire. She hadn't even recognized his voice. He had just seemed like a normal guy, until he turned on the charm.

"That she obviously doesn't, Jimmy," he said.

"Wait...are you...Rob Blake?" she asked.

He reached around Sandra and shook Angie's hand. "Yeah, but don't tell anybody about it. Check it out." He stretched his jaw and pulled out a pair of cheek pads. "Sandra taught me how to do my makeup, so I don't look like myself. It makes a great disguise."

"No kidding," Angie said in a strangled voice. She was turning fangirl all the sudden, barely able to get a word out of her tight-locked throat.

"So logically...this must be your stunt double," Angie said.

"Jim Urban, bookstore lady. Bookstore lady, my stunt double, Jim Urban."

"Hi," she said, getting up to shake Jim Urban's hand. Angie flashed back to seeing Rob and Jim at the Chamber of Commerce a few days ago. Rob had said that he needed the name of a realtor. *Ohh,* Angie thought. This guy was one of Hollywood's biggest stars! If he wanted to buy a house on Nantucket at the drop of a hat, he could. She felt like an idiot. "Boy, my face must be red."

"Don't worry about it," he said.

"Where's your sister?" Rob asked Sandra, as Angie was sitting down.

Sandra rolled her eyes. "Probably still in her room, crying her eyes out and forcing Lucy to wait on her hand and foot. She should be glad the man's dead."

"Harsh," Rob Blake, who had been named Handsomest Man in America in 2012 by *Time* magazine, said. "But you're not wrong."

"Wait," Angie gasped. "Julia Withers is your sister?"

"Yup," Sandra said. "How do you think I got this job? She insists on only working with me. She always has."

Rob said, "You know what? By this time tomorrow, she's going to have her armor on. You would never know that Lance Mitchell was the so-called love of her life. She's got control. She was probably more upset during that scene we were practicing in her room the other day."

Sandra said drily, "I think you freaked out her assistant."

"Why?"

"I heard she thought it was Lance Mitchell in there, bellowing at my sister."

Rob guffawed, leaning back so hard in his chair that he almost tipped over. "What a mouse! If she'd put her ear at the door she would have heard me calling Julia by her character's name and ranting about how I wasn't really a man anymore with all those injuries! 'Amanda, how can you love someone like me? I'm ruined!' Honestly. If you're gonna listen at doors, at least do a good job about it."

Angie, putting some pieces together very quickly, said, "Was this Sunday night? At about eleven?"

"Yeah, just after everyone else left for the night. We were supposed to film it on Monday. We'll probably have to film it in a couple of days, though. We should rehearse again. *Or* I could send in my stunt double. Nobody would notice, right?"

He winked at Angie, obviously teasing her.

Angie shook her head. "I would never have guessed you were sisters. I thought Rob and Jim were twins, though."

That got another laugh out of everyone.

They tried to keep up the conversation, but it was clear—to Angie, at least—that she was still freaked out over Rob Blake's arrival, and she wasn't going to be able to get over it any time soon. She excused herself after a few minutes of increasingly big yawns. It was after midnight, and she was an up-before-dawn kind of girl.

And, in the morning, she would have to open the bookstore. On her own. Janet had the morning off.

She let one of the VW Microbus drivers take her home. Three strong screwdrivers in a row had left her worried that she would do something dumb like drive off the road. She was such a lightweight! She would have to send Janet out with the bicycle to pick up her car when she went out to do the book deliveries for the store later that afternoon.

She yawned again, trying to remember how she survived staying up all night in high school. It had never seemed like a big deal back then. An extra cup of coffee used to take care of everything.

Now? She'd be lucky if she didn't sleep through her alarm.

# Chapter 12

# BAD ASSUMPTIONS

Wednesday morning came all too quickly, with Angie waking up even earlier than usual. She had gone to bed worried that she would oversleep, and the alarm had awakened her from a nightmare in which she was trying to make coffee for her customers, only to have them shatter their mugs on the floor, yelling about how terrible the coffee was. She was almost glad to be awake.

She got up and started on her usual morning routine. Showered, dressed, and with a fresh pot of coffee in the insulated carafe for Aunt Margery when she woke up later, she stepped outside. The morning was cool but clear. It was going to be a bright, sunny April day, perfect for filming.

She walked over to her car in the driveway and stopped. It was gone. She almost slapped herself on the forehead; her car was still out at the beach.

And...there was really something she needed deal with before she did anything else that day, even if it meant she couldn't open the store, she realized. Something that she needed to talk over with someone, to make sure she wasn't going completely nuts.

She didn't want to wake Aunt Margery. She still wasn't ready for the kind of analysis that her great-aunt would lay down on her half-formed theories.

She bit her lip, then gave the police station a call. "Are Mickey and Jo Jerritt still there?"

The officer who had answered her call said, "Yes, ma'am."

"It's Angie Prouty. Are there, uh, visiting hours? Can I see them? I want to ask them something."

There was a pause. The officer said, "You can see Mickey Jerritt, if you like. Jo Jerritt is asleep."

"Whatever you do, don't wake her," Angie said. "I'll be right over."

She changed shoes and got her bike out, then rode over to the police station. Mickey was up and pacing his cell. An officer opened the door for her and left the door open, sitting out in the hallway. It was clear that, once again, they weren't expecting an escape attempt. Angie couldn't help but think that the police officers thought that the arrest was just as bunkum as she did.

"Hey," Mickey said when he saw her. "Glad to see you. That was a long night."

Angie's heart broke as she looked Mickey over. He had dark circles under his eyes and his hair looked dirty and tousled. She felt like she'd failed him.

Angie gave him a warm hug. "I'm sorry I don't have you freed yet."

Mickey held onto the hug and then let go, looking into Angie's eyes with a faint smile. "I know you're working on it. Not too worried."

"You look worried."

"Nah, just impatient."

Angie sat on the edge of the cot to try to encourage him to sit down and chill out, but he kept pacing back and forth in the small cell. "I usually have most of the baking for the day done by now, you know? What are you doing for pastries this morning? Are you going to be okay?"

"I'll work something out," she said.

"Call Callahan's Grocery and get them to save all their pastries for you. They're not as good as mine, but hey, at least they don't come out of a plastic wrapper."

"Thanks, I will." She felt awkward. When she had awakened that morning, it had felt like she had figured something out. But now that it came to saying it out loud, she felt like she had nothing but hot air.

"So...what's up?" Mickey asked.

"I came up with a list of suspects and I need a sanity check," Angie admitted. "Am I going crazy or do these people actually sound reasonable? That's what I need to know."

"And you decided to run them past me?" Mickey said. "Why me?"

He sounded suspicious and wary.

"Honestly, because everyone else I could think of would have just poked holes in everything I said," Angie said.

"Harsh," Mickey said. "But yeah...your great-aunt is like that. So is Jo."

"At least, that's what it feels like this morning. I needed someone, um, a little more supportive."

Mickey chuckled, then lay down on the cot, swinging his legs in behind her. He put his arms behind his head and closed his eyes. "Okay, lay it on me. I'm listening."

Angie blew air out of her cheeks. "Here's my problem. Everyone in town *and* on the film crew already knows that I'm looking into the murders. If I ask the actual questions that I need to ask to solve this, the whole island will find out."

"True."

"And most of the people who want me to solve this case don't really care if it gets solved. They just want the problem to go away."

"Yeah...count me in that group. I honestly don't care who did it. I'm just sick of being locked up because of it."

"But," Angie said, "I don't work like that. I can't solve a case knowing that I have to treat justice as less important than convenience."

"Then don't," Mickey said. "I mean, solve it, but solve it your way. They'll just have to deal with the fact that you are on the case and you're going to do as good a job as you can on it."

"I'm going to make some people mad."

He opened his eyes and grinned at her. "People are going to get mad anyway. Customers, am I right? They're kind of irrational. Think about everyone on the island as being like...customers of justice!"

She rolled her eyes and tried to suppress a snort.

"So who are your suspects?" he asked. "Me and Jo, obviously."

She shook her head. "You and Jo had no real reason to kill Lance Mitchell. He just isn't important enough to either of you. He said something mean to me and set you off the other night, but you've never been the kind of guy to lash out at people when they make you angry."

Even as a kid, Mickey hadn't been interested in getting back at other people. Revenge wasn't his gig.

Mickey didn't answer for a moment. "You know that anyone who screws with you is in for trouble though, right?"

"You didn't do it, did you?" Angie asked.

"Well, no, I mean, the guy was obviously his own worst karma."

"You see my point?"

Mickey made a face. "Yeah, okay. I look before I leap, at least when it comes to violence. But what about Jo?"

Angie giggled. "Oh, man. If Jo was going to kill someone, she'd do it with her fists."

Mickey said, "Do you remember that one time she beat up Amy Spencer in third grade for trying to steal your lunch money?"

"I do. Like it was yesterday. She was always in trouble for getting into fistfights."

"She loves confrontations," Mickey agreed. "Poison? Not Jo. Flamethrower, maybe. So, who *do you* have as suspects, if it's not us?"

"Let's talk about my logic first, so you can see why I came up with the ones I did."

"Okay."

"The kind of person who commits a poisoning is a real planning type. Poisoning isn't something you do in the heat of the moment. It's something you think out ahead of time, like, *hmmm, I wonder how I could kill someone without getting caught?*"

"Following you so far."

"An actor would be an ideal poisoner, actually," Angie said. "Someone who could carry out the crime and then believably act their way through the aftermath. I've been researching poisoners. Convicted poisoners tend to be manipulative. They were raised in unhappy homes and tend to be emotionally stunted, the kind of people who would do something just because they had been told no. Poisoners are the kind of people who, when they can't get their way, just smile and pretend it doesn't bother them. And then they go into planning mode."

"I know some people like that," Mickey said.

"These are people who hate confrontations, yet who can't stand to compromise, either. They want what they want with a minimum of fuss. Money. Freedom from people who are quote-unquote holding them back. Revenge for perceived slights. That kind of thing."

"It sounds incredibly petty," Mickey said.

"I know, right? And another thing. If it was the cupcake that was used to poison Lance Mitchell, I mean, I'm just going to assume that for now even though we haven't proven it yet, then that points toward familiarity with the guy. They knew Lance had a sweet tooth."

"And, you know. It might be kind of a commentary on how self-indulgent he was," Mickey said. "If he hadn't been such a greedy bastard, he might not have died. Whoever did it knew he wasn't about to share those cupcakes."

"And...whoever did it may have had a familiarity with cooking or baking to be able to put the poison inside the cupcake."

"Huh?" Mickey asked. "You just take a piping bag or a syringe or something, jab it into the cupcake under the frosting and into the middle, then smooth the frosting back down."

"Right, but how many people know that?"

He shrugged.

"So, all things considered, I have four main suspects. None of them am I even remotely sure about. So do *not* take any of these people seriously, and don't tell the cops."

"Check."

Almost whispering, she said, "My first suspects are Jeanette and Sheldon."

She could see him biting back a snap response.

Angie continued, "It's a crazy coincidence, but Jeanette knew Lance in France. I'm assuming that Sheldon, being part of the same circle, knew him too. It seems that there was bad blood between Sheldon and Lance at some point. Both Jeanette and Sheldon know about baking and had access to the movie set."

Mickey said, "Anyone who had access to the set had a reasonably safe shot at poisoning the cupcakes, though. Everyone on the set knew that Lance was going to hog all the cupcakes and throw a fit if anyone else took any. And are Jeanette or Sheldon the kind of people who could poison somebody?"

"First, Jeanette and Sheldon probably have access to poison for the restaurant. You have to, to kill off any pests," Angie said. "But as far as the ability to poison someone? Sheldon's not much of a planner.

Jeanette's the one who runs the books and makes sure they don't go broke."

"Fair point. But can you really see Jeanette putting the back of her hand to her forehead and saying, 'The world isn't what I wish it to be...I think I'll change it a little to make sure that I get the revenge that I've always wanted but have never mentioned to anyone before now,'?"

"No," Angie said. "I mean, Sheldon's always been the more melodramatic of the two of them, but even he wouldn't say that."

"You're really just trying to be fair about the murder having been done by someone on the island, aren't you?" Mickey said.

Angie had already wiped Mickey and Jo off the books as suspects, which made her feel slightly guilty. Mickey was spot on.

She sighed. "What does it say about me that I could suspect either of them for a moment?"

He just laughed at her. "Oh, you're a terrible person. The worst. That's two suspects. Who else?"

"Al Petrillo."

"Al Petrillo? The Red Sox fan?"

Angie explained that Al was the camera operator, a creative type who had been hurt by Lance Mitchell. Lance Mitchell had *humiliated* him. Al seemed to be pretty good at coming up with unusual murder scenarios when they had talked at the bonfire. He had been on the set, too.

"But is Al the kind of person who would poison someone?" Mickey asked.

"I don't know," Angie admitted. "He tries to avoid confrontation. He seems nice, but someone who's putting on an act can seem nice, too. Like Doug McConnell."

Doug McConnell was the man she had dated before Walter who had stolen her ideas and claimed them as his own, had treated her like dirt, and had cheated on her. She had come up with a thousand reasons for him to act the way he had. It had seemed to her, until she finally gave up on the jerk, that he could do no wrong. He had seemed just as surprised as she had been when she actually figured it out. He *loved* stringing her along.

Mickey glowered. "Now, there's a guy I'd like to let Jo have a few moments alone with."

Angie laughed.

"But you don't have anything more solid than that?" Mickey asked.

She shook her head.

"Okay. Last one?"

"Julia Withers, the lead actress."

She explained about the relationship that Julia and Lance had together, and about Lucy Smith trying to coach her into having the strength to face the press after Lance's death.

Angie said, "Clearly Julia had reasons for wanting Lance Mitchell dead."

Mickey said, "Clearly she had access to the set on Saturday while the cupcakes were there."

"Clearly she has the kind of personality where she wants to avoid conflict."

Mickey waggled his eyebrows. "Clearly she's an actress."

Angie rolled her eyes.

"And," Mickey added, "what if she and Lance were secretly married? Then she would inherit all his wealth. The secret marriage plot, that's a thing."

"Or she might have just been written into his will," Angie said. "No need to turn this into a soap opera."

"How is this *not* a soap opera?" Mickey asked.

Angie had watched Julia transform from a woman who was freaking out to a woman who was completely calm and controlled, at Lucy Smith's direction.

*Wait...*

Angie shook her head. She had forgotten to examine her assumptions again.

"What is it? You thought of something?" Mickey said.

"I have to add two more suspects."

"Who?"

"Lucy Smith and Lloyd Rapinski. I had initially ruled out Lucy because she seemed like she didn't care about anything other than her boss and had blown off all the drama between Julia and Lance."

"But...?"

"But had she really? Maybe she had known how it would go between them. She was so sure of how Lance would behave that she had assumed that she was hearing Lance and Julia fight in Julia's room earlier that night, when it was really her and Rob rehearsing the scene. She *could* have poisoned the cupcakes to get back at Lance for hurting Julia. Maybe it was *her* father that was the noted chemist."

Mickey said, "Someday you're going to tell me all about this. You just said a bunch of things that I don't understand because I was locked up in jail."

"Sorry," she said.

"Don't explain it now. Just run with it. That covers Lucy Smith. What about the other one?"

"Lloyd Rapinski, Lance's personal assistant. I had mentally cleared Lloyd earlier because he had an alibi for the time that Lance Mitchell had been in his room that evening. But he would have had access to the Saturday cupcakes while they were on the set."

"And a motive...for murder!" Mickey added.

Angie smacked her forehead. "Ugh, never mind. I forgot that the cupcakes on the set, the Saturday ones, would have gone stale by Sunday. Lance ate the poisoned cupcake on Sunday and died on Sunday. If he had eaten the cupcake on Saturday he would have died on *Saturday*, not Sunday! Now I have to work out who could have poisoned the cupcakes on Sunday... Who could have gotten the key to unlock his room? This is nuts. I'm never going to be able to get you out of here."

Mickey took a deep breath. "Okay, hang on a minute. There are a whole lot of cupcakes involved here."

Angie tried hard not to crack a smile. This was just like Mickey, always able to cheer her up.

"So, let me get this straight," he continued. "You think the cupcakes that killed Lance were the ones he bought from our bakery? The ones he came in to buy on Sunday?"

Angie nodded weakly. "I'm sorry, Mickey. This is the best I've got for now."

"Don't worry about it," Mickey said. He gave her a weak smile.

"I *am* worried about it," Angie said. "I can't leave you in here!"

"Hey, Jo and I aren't going to go broke over a week in the slammer. And you're not screwing anything up. It's just gonna take some time to get this all sorted out. If it was straightforward, the case would have been closed already. It's only been a few days. Give yourself some time." Mickey reached over to touch Angie's shoulder, looking into her eyes.

Angie felt a spark of electricity pass between the two. Suddenly, she bolted up from the cot. "Mickey. I just thought of something else. The ferries from the mainland to the island don't have crap for security. The poisoner could have brought the poison with them onto the island, just in case there was an opportunity to get to Lance. They didn't have to get it from anywhere on the island at all."

"I thought you said that poisoners were planners."

"Maybe they did plan this," Angie said. "Just very, very quickly."

After leaving the police station, Angie followed Mickey's advice about getting the pastries from Callahan's. They were willing to sell...but they weren't willing to deliver until eight a.m., and even then, she had to promise to pay the driver a huge tip. It was the best she could do.

She put a sign on the door: *Save Mickey and Jo! No pastries today until 8 a.m. or later.*

Then she made herself a double-shot of espresso, buried it in a cup of strong coffee with about a quarter cup of cream, and turned the door sign from "closed" to "open."

Her regulars appeared like magic. They grumbled about the lack of pastries, but in a good-natured way that was more about complaining that the police were being pressured to arrest someone—anyone—in order to make the Hollywood bigwigs happy, than it was about her not being able to sell them Nantucket Bakery bear claws to go with their coffee.

One of them stood up and read the *Boston Herald*'s article on the ongoing investigations. There was a profile of Lance Mitchell that made him out to be a *character* rather than a complete jerk. There was also a short statement from Detective Bailey stating that two persons of interest in the case were currently being held for investigation, very professional and noncommittal.

Loud "boos" filled the room after the reading of the article.

At eight, the pastries arrived, looking edible but not up to Mickey and Jo's standards. The regulars seemed disinclined to purchase them, which made her feel ironically satisfied, even though she had paid way too much money to get them delivered in the first place. Maybe she could foist them off on some tourists. No, that was the wrong attitude to take. Tourists kept her in business! She was just in a bad mood from still being slightly hung over and not having enough sleep.

Aunt Margery walked in at ten a.m., just as Angie's phone rang. She pulled up her stool and took over on the café register while Angie pinned her cell phone to her shoulder as she pulled a double-shot of espresso.

"Hello? Angie speaking. I mean, Pastries & Page-Turners, how may I help you with all your book, caffeine, and carb needs?"

She was getting silly. Maybe she should take a nap.

It was Detective Bailey. "Miss Prouty, do you have a moment? I'd like to see you at the police station."

That didn't sound good. "If I can get Aunt Margery settled in, I should be able to come over in about half an hour? Will that be okay?"

"That should be fine," he said agreeably and hung up.

In their previous conversations about the case, he hadn't had any problems telling her things he shouldn't have over the phone. It must be something major, something he wanted to make sure she wouldn't repeat to anyone else.

Burning with curiosity, she forced herself to check everything over in the bookstore so that Aunt Margery wouldn't have any issues while she was gone.

"What do you think it's about?" Aunt Margery asked.

"Either something that makes Jo or Mickey look guilty, something that completely blows all our previous ideas out of the water, or something that will make the whole island look bad," she said. "Or all three."

"Well, you have *that* to look forward to, then," said her great-aunt.

Angie arrived at the police station on her bicycle, her car still being out at the beach. The officer at the front desk escorted her to Detective Bailey's office. He was on the phone. He waved at the door and she closed it. She sat in the chair across from him, feeling a little bit like a kid who'd been called into the principal's office.

"Yes, I understand that it will take some time to get permission to access their medical histories and that your workload is such that we can't be moved up in the process. I'm sure that it won't be a problem. Thank you."

Detective Bailey hung up the phone as if he had been commenting on the time of day with an old friend, then turned to her. "Miss Prouty. Thank you for coming."

"That sounded like a frustrating call," Angie said.

"It was," he said. "I've been trying to keep a better hold on my temper."

"What did you want to see me about?"

He took a deep breath. "I'm afraid I have some very trying news for you, which you will need to keep under your belt. The lab results on what was in Lance Mitchell's stomach have come back early."

"And?"

"He wasn't poisoned."

Angie leaned back in the chair. She couldn't breathe.

"Not technically, at least," Detective Bailey amended. "He died of an allergic reaction to penicillin."

"He wasn't murdered?" Angie asked, her jaw falling slack.

"Not necessarily. A large amount of liquid penicillin *was* in his stomach. He wasn't killed by cyanide, but it was clearly a planned event."

"I'm sorry, Detective Bailey, but are you sure?" Angie's mind flashed back to what Al had told her about the red rash on Lance's body, such a common side effect of cyanide poisoning.

"I am sure, Angie. Cyanide was not used to murder Lance Mitchell."

Angie could feel her heart drop, realizing she had been wrong about the cyanide this whole time. A white hot wave of embarrassment washed over her. Detective Bailey gave her a sympathetic smile, which only made her feel worse. Angie couldn't believe she hadn't double checked the rash theory.

Bailey cleared his throat.

"So, any luck tracking down who did it?" he asked.

"I'm not sure," she admitted. "This new fact changes everything. I'll need time to think about it. Just now, were you asking someone to check the movie crew's medical records to make sure none of them had a penicillin prescription?"

Detective Bailey nodded.

Angie sighed. "I might as well tell you what I'm thinking, although you've probably been thinking the same things." Angie told him about her suspects, even Jeanette and Sheldon.

"I feel kind of gross for suspecting them," she added. "And I'm still not sure what to think, now that I've ruled out the first box of cupcakes."

"The cupcakes had all been eaten, by the way. Both boxes in the room were empty. There was one with a pink and green ribbon and one without. Nothing but crumbs in either, and a lot of wrappers in the trash can."

"What a glutton! He didn't look like he was the kind of guy to eat that much. He must have had a metabolism like a horse."

Detective Bailey said, "If it makes you feel any better about what you said about Jeanette and Sheldon, well, you're not alone in feeling a little disgusted with yourself. But you have to suspect everyone fairly, even the people you like."

"I thought I had a fairly good track record of doing that," she said. The two previous investigations that she had butted in on had involved people she still couldn't comprehend as killers. She had known them too long for that.

"Yes, you do. But you're always closer to some people than others."

"So...Penicillin?" she repeated.

"Anaphylaxis," Detective Bailey said. "His throat swelled shut and he choked to death. Apparently it's rare in reactions to penicillin, but it can happen. Mitchell was unlucky."

Suddenly suspicious, she said, "You didn't think it was cyanide in the first place, did you?"

"I wasn't prepared to make an assumption like that."

"If you don't make some assumptions in a situation like this, you can't even get started sorting out who could have done it," she said.

The detective tilted his head to the side. Even though they had both grown up on the island, they didn't know each other as well as she and Jo and Mickey did. He was older than she was and had always seemed about a thousand times more professional.

"I would tend to agree with you in theory, but in practice it always seems to turn out wrong," he said. "When you're solving some types of puzzles, you just have to make an educated guess and go from there. If the puzzle all fits together, then you've guessed right. If it doesn't, then you just start over. But with police work, you have to be careful about your guesses. You only really get one chance to solve a crime like this. Let's say we worked out who the murderer was, but in the course of making our guess, we made some bad assumptions. Or, even if we happened to jump straight to the *right* conclusions, but without getting every piece of evidence we needed to make a solid case, we might end up with the jury telling us that the suspect wasn't guilty beyond a reasonable doubt. At that point, our hands would be tied. There is no second try."

"So, you're saying you don't make any assumptions? Or that you handle them differently?"

"I think it's more that we handle them differently than most people would," he said. "Ideally, if you're a good police officer, you're willing to be wrong."

"Wrong about what?"

"Oh, pretty much everything," he said. "Not willing to *do* wrong, of course, just willing to change your mind about things."

"Are you trying to give me a hint?" she asked.

"No," he said. "Just making conversation, that's all. Not many folks are interested in actually investigating a crime. They just want to make it disappear. As long as the problem goes away, they don't actually care how it happened."

She snorted. "I may have been thinking something along those lines earlier."

"And, since it's pretty obvious that I'm not going to be able to convince you not to get involved in this sort of thing on a regular basis, it's better to make sure I can keep an eye on you."

"Is that why you're telling me this stuff? Because I'm pretty sure you shouldn't be."

"You were going to find out anyway. Question is, will you hang onto your bad assumptions longer than you have to?"

# Chapter 13

## INTUITIVE JUMPS

Penicillin.

She had been so sure—without any sort of experience in investigating poisonings whatsoever, that Lance Mitchell had been poisoned. But it had been penicillin.

Who could possibly have known he was allergic?

Any of them. The change in method didn't rule out any of her suspects. Jeanette could have known because she had known the man personally, back in the day. Sheldon could have found out from Jeanette.

No, wait. It couldn't have been either of them, because they couldn't have tampered with the cupcakes on Sunday. Her head was spinning.

Julia would be the most likely to know. But then again, it could have been gossip traded around the industry.

The thing about penicillin was that it would be even easier to get than cyanide, but it would leave a prescription trail behind, unless of course the killer had stolen someone else's penicillin to leave a false trail.

Not having the willpower to go back to the bookstore and explain to Aunt Margery that she had been dead wrong about the cause of death, and had basically been called to the mat about it by Detective Bailey, Angie decided to at least do something productive by rescuing her car. She pedaled the miles to Nobadeer Beach while quietly kicking herself for just accepting the information she was given. Next time she would double check her assumptions.

It was a beautiful day for biking: sunny, breezy, not too hot.

The beach had been cleaned up, but not perfectly. She could see where the pit for the clambake had been dug and the pile of burned seaweed had been dumped afterwards. The wood from the bonfire had been dragged off, but the soot and coals remained.

She fastened her bike onto her VW Golf's bike rack, then walked out onto the sand.

Penicillin.

Not cyanide.

What other bad assumptions had she made?

She had assumed that the killer would be difficult to find, for one thing, and that everyone had a motive for killing him, at the very least for being rude. But was that really true?

Aunt Margery loved to quote that old P.D. James line to her, "All the motives for murder are covered by four Ls: Love, Lust, Lucre and Loathing." Which really didn't include somebody being rude.

Sane people had to have more of a motivation to murder than just thinking that someone was a jerk. Loathing? The kind of loathing that became murderous hate took something more significant than mere rudeness. *She* didn't want to kill Lance Mitchell, and he definitely had been rude to her. Hollywood bigwigs were famous for being difficult to work with. As far as most of the film crew was concerned, Lance Mitchell was just one more bad boss in an otherwise good career.

So, who had an *actual* motive to kill him?

She pedaled back to the bookstore, frustrated but feeling better. Watching the ocean had a tendency to put her problems in perspective. Her two best friends were basically being framed for murder for the convenience of some Hollywood bigwigs who didn't want to lose money on a stupid TV movie. Everyone was expecting her to solve the mystery, moving the accusation of murder from her two best friends to someone more acceptable to both the island and to Hollywood itself. She was still about a million miles from solving the case, and she had already been horribly wrong about so many things that it was obvious that she was in over her head. Trying to solve the case was useless, and she should just stop. But, despite all that, she wasn't going to. She was too nosy and too stubborn.

Sometimes the perspective that she gained from watching the ocean wasn't the most flattering.

Aunt Margery was struggling to keep up with a sudden rush of customers. Angie stepped in to work the espresso machine.

"Just the two of us," she said. "Just like old times."

"I much prefer the days when Janet's here," Aunt Margery said.

"Down with the old times! Hooray for the new times!" Angie said.

Aunt Margery gave her one of her looks, one that said, *don't get smart with me, I can still outsmart you faster than you can slam your buzzer on a Jeopardy question.* "What did Detective Bailey have to say?"

Once again, Angie was struck with the urge not to tell her great-aunt everything. Not because she wished to keep it secret, but because the information didn't feel ripe yet.

"I screwed something up and he wanted to make sure that I knew it," Angie said, not quite untruthfully. "I'll tell you about it later. He doesn't want it spread around."

She would tell Aunt Margery all about it after the case was solved. The truth was, Aunt Margery would spread the fact that it hadn't been cyanide all over town. Discreetly, only to people she trusted... but someone would leak.

And one of the people she would tell was Sheldon.

Aunt Margery gave her another look, a more speculative one. "He's telling you things that haven't been publicly released yet, isn't he?"

Angie bit her lip and nodded.

"And you don't trust me?"

"I do. But I promised."

Aunt Margery had strange ideas about what could and could not be told to one's great-aunt if a promise not to say anything had been made. Her nostrils twitched as if she could smell the secret trying to jump off Angie's tongue.

Another customer came in, and Angie said, "What's your order?"

"Cappuccino."

She started the drink, leaving Aunt Margery to deal with the payment. When she was done, she did a sweep of the bookstore, making sure that all was in order.

Lance Mitchell's film book had been returned to its shelf. Because the shelves were so depleted, Aunt Margery had faced the book outward on a wire rack next to a modest stack of copies of another book.

*Delusions of Filmmaking,* by Anonymous.

The new book was none other than the fictionalized Hollywood tell-all, and Aunt Margery had set it right next to Lance Mitchell's book.

Angie grabbed the top-most copy and brought it back to the counter. "I'm going to reread this. Will you be okay for another hour or two?"

"Bribe me with a sandwich and I'm yours."

Angie walked downtown to Aunt Margery's favorite deli and picked up a toasted club sandwich for her, and a patty melt for herself. The kid at the counter, someone she didn't even know, asked, "Solve the murder yet?" with a huge grin on his face.

"Not yet."

She dropped off her great-aunt's sandwich at the coffee counter, then decided to hole up in the break room at the back of the store. She needed the comfort of her favorite armchair to help her power through the book.

Angie ended up rereading the book in one sitting, barely noticing that her legs had fallen asleep until she tried to get up to stretch.

Her brain was ticking.

So, *Delusions of Filmmaking: A Novel of a Dirty Rotten Hollywood Scoundrel* had almost certainly been written by the person who had co-written Lance Mitchell's book *Nouvelle Vague: How the French Broke*

*Free of Psychological Realism with New Wave Cinema, 1958–1969*. Or, at least, by someone who claimed to have done so, in pretty damning detail.

Coincidentally, whoever had written *Delusions of Filmmaking* had placed the main character in the hospital due to an infection from a cut on his foot. In the scene, the character had discovered that he was allergic to penicillin. He had screamed angrily at the nurses, fearing that he would have to have the foot amputated. He had been such a bastard that he had been transferred from that hospital to another one entirely, almost causing a traffic accident in the ambulance by attacking a paramedic along the way.

How was she supposed to narrow down suspects now? The book had come out two weeks ago. Anyone even remotely connected to Lance Mitchell would have had the chance to read it.

And would know that he was allergic to penicillin.

The copyright page gave away nothing. The copyright was held by the publisher, probably in trust for the author.

It might be possible for someone who knew the film industry well to identify the author by cross-referencing who had worked with whom, and who had been part of the film circle in France, et cetera. But Angie didn't have that kind of time. Not to mention the fact that it would be dangerous for her to start asking those kinds of questions. If she tried asking someone from the movie crew she might end up asking the murderer themselves.

Who killed Lance Mitchell? She felt like she was beating her head against a wall.

She took a deep breath and settled back onto the armchair. She was trying to force herself to come up with an intuitive jump. But intuitive jumps never worked that way. They couldn't be forced. It wasn't possible to write all the facts down, set them in order, and then *bam*, expect to solve the case right there.

Angie could spend the rest of the year trying to push herself to come up with the right answer.

Or she could do things the way she normally did them and wait for something to pop out at her.

She needed to trust herself. Just because this was a Hollywood murder that her friends were being framed for didn't mean it was more or less important than the other two murders she had investigated. Murder was still the taking of a human life, the result of the decision that violence, either planned or unplanned, was a perfectly valid answer to the question of "how do I make this inconvenient problem go away?"

And that remained *wrong*. But her two best friends being unfairly held in jail cells for a murder they most certainly did not commit was wrong, too.

Angie released a loud, exasperated sigh and threw her head back against the armchair.

"Angie, dear, is everything okay in here?" It was Aunt Margery, peering cautiously into to the break room. She saw Angie, sprawled across the chair, *Delusions of Filmmaking* thrown over her lap while *Nouvelle Vague* sat open on the floor. Aunt Margery gave her great-niece a gentle smile and walked over to her.

Angie glanced up at her from her position on the chair. "No. Everything is not okay. I have no idea what I'm doing. I need to get my best friends out of jail and I'm sitting here getting nothing done." Angie felt almost completely beaten down in this moment.

"Oh, sweetheart, you put so much pressure on yourself."

What Aunt Margery didn't seem to understand was exactly how much of a high-pressure situation this was. Angie knew it, and it seemed that almost everyone else on the island did, too.

"I just want to figure out who did this," Angie said.

"I know you do. Your drive and passion are some of your greatest strengths. In many ways, you remind me of your mother right now."

Angie's head whipped up as she looked at Aunt Margery. "You never mention my mother. Why now?"

"Well, maybe you need a little inspiration from her. You two are more alike than you think."

"Ha, ha. Very funny. My mother, the vagabond who decided to open a hotel in Florida and me – I couldn't even last five years off the island before I came back. I appreciate the sentiment but I really need to get back to work," Angie said with a slight eye roll. Although they were distant, she loved her parents. But she would never say they had much in common.

"Just think about it, Angie. Yes, she and your father went to Florida, but it's because they crave *adventure*. Just like how you turn to your books. Our family really tends to lean toward escapism, eh?"

"Yeah, yeah. I guess."

Aunt Margery smiled to herself. "Remember this, my dear. Happy families are all alike; every unhappy family is unhappy in its own way."

"Yes, Tolstoy. I know that one."

"Whether you believe it or not, you are so similar to your parents.

Their passions, their loves, their hobbies – they have been passed down to you. In that way, you are all alike. Yes, the Proutys certainly have our idiosyncrasies. But we've got a lot of good amongst us, too. Your mother's fierce loyalty, your father's brains... You have it within you to solve this."

Aunt Margery bent down to gently kiss Angie on the top of her head. She winked at her great-niece and retreated from the break room.

## Chapter 14

## FAMILY CONNECTIONS

*Happy families are all alike; every unhappy family is unhappy in its own way.*

Angie couldn't stop replaying this quote again and again in her head. She began pacing around the break room, biting a hang nail off her thumb. Was it true? How much did she really have in common with her parents? She thought of her bookstore, the one venture in her life that she was most proud of. Yes, she supposed that there was some truth to what Aunt Margery had said. Books were a route of escape for her, and by opening the bookstore she had hoped to provide others with that same experience. Maybe her parents' travels were their ways of escaping, too.

Angie smiled, imagining her parents at the hotel they opened in Florida. She realized that the Proutys certainly had a knack for entrepreneurship, too.

Looking around the room, Angie's eyes flickered over to her family's most prized possession – a large oak bookshelf with ornate engraved detail. Before Angie even signed the lease agreement for her store, she knew her family's bookshelf had to have a home there. While the entire store was crammed from floor to ceiling with books, this one shelf was an exception. It was filled with trinkets, photo albums, and other memorabilia from Angie's childhood.

Angie walked over to the bookshelf and swept her fingers across the cover of some photo albums. She grabbed one, flipping through it and smiling to herself. There were pictures of her, her parents, Aunt Margery, all enjoying various seasons on the island. Swimming at Children's Beach, pumpkin carving at the farm, building snowmen in the front yard.

She glanced down at one picture of her mother in their kitchen, undoubtedly baking her infamous cinnamon buns for Angie, Jo, and Mickey. How many hours did Angie herself now spend behind the café counter, ensuring each of her customer's stomachs were happily filled?

Seeing a photo of her father behind his desk, posing with a beaten copy of a James Patterson novel, made her smile. The same novel was ironically one of the many books that turned her into such an avid reader. She often forgot about these moments, the little things that made her a Prouty. She was more of her parents than she realized.

*Wait.*

Parents. Similarities.

*Nouvelle Vague.* The chemist father. Angie ran back over to where the book sat on her armchair and flipped furiously to the endnotes. And there it was, right in front of Angie's face.

"To shout *fire* in a crowded theater is like announcing that a bomb is about to go off...That's how my father, a noted chemist, explained it to me..." Angie stared at "chemist," her jaw slack.

What was it that Aunt Margery had said? You are your parents?

Angie gasped and threw her photo album onto the floor.

Angie stepped out of the back room and found Aunt Margery sitting behind her antique desk typing away furiously at something on the computer. She had let her tea get cold. Angie made her another cuppa and dumped out the old one, putting the porcelain cup in the dirty dish bin.

"How was your family research, dear?" Her great-aunt asked with a smile.

"Um...Productive," Angie said.

"Have you solved the murder yet?"

"I may have."

"Oh, who? One of the locals, a member of the film crew, or someone else entirely?"

"I'm going to have to talk about it with Detective Bailey before I say anything. We should probably close the bookstore, too, in case I'm right. I want the bookstore locked up, with one of Detective Bailey's deputies watching it, and you safe at home before I talk to him."

That earned her a tilt of the head and a thoughtful look. "You're taking this seriously, then?"

Angie chewed on her bottom lip for a moment. "I am. I still don't feel like anyone should consider me the unofficial island sleuth or anything like that, but I seem to have a talent for answering questions that other people seem to think are impossible to answer. To me it doesn't really feel like anything special."

"But it is," Aunt Margery said.

"I guess." Angie responded. "But I also know that I don't trust anyone else to do it."

"Not even Detective Bailey?"

"I think he does a good job," Angie said, "but he doesn't have the same insights that I do. What he does is right for him, and right for making sure that criminals actually have jail time to face. But, what I do is right for the island, too. Everyone wants those who are inconveniently guilty to be protected, because they're a part of the community. But they also know, somewhere in the back of their minds, that that isn't good for anyone in the long term. Some secrets shouldn't be kept. The rocks have to be rolled back and all the crawly things underneath exposed to the light."

"I hope that you don't mean that someone we're close to did it," Aunt Margery said. She had a tight look on her face.

"You hope that," Angie said. "But is that what you really want? For it to just go away? It never works like that. The wrong people get blamed, everyone gets paranoid, and we all start to suspect each other."

Aunt Margery sighed. "No...no. I *hope* it isn't anyone important to me. But it still has to be done."

Angie leaned over and kissed her great-aunt on the temple. "Thank you. As long as I know that you, at least, understand that this needs to be done, no matter who is involved, then I can do this. And...just to set your mind at rest, no. It wasn't one of the locals. At least, I'm pretty sure it wasn't."

Aunt Margery's shoulders slumped with relief. "I apologize for not always having seen that. For wanting to protect you from accusing the wrong people."

"Apology accepted. After all, your little Tolstoy quote may have solved the case." Angie gave her aunt a little smirk, and before she had to answer any more questions, told Aunt Margery it was time to go home.

After Angie discussed the plans for the night, Aunt Margery promised to go straight home, make a frozen lasagna from the freezer, and keep the doors locked and her cell phone next to her at all times. Angie believed that she would do it too, for tonight at least.

Angie cleaned up the store, putting it to rights. It wasn't really that important to get it all done, although it would have been inconvenient later if she hadn't. It was just that cleaning and putting things in order, both physically and with her orders and receipts and the various pieces of paperwork that kept her little ship afloat, was a way to put her ideas about the murderer in order as well.

The work she did as she closed for the evening was to turn her intuition into a solid theory, one that she wouldn't be completely embarrassed to put in front of Detective Bailey.

But the fact remained that she needed to collect a few more pieces of evidence to prove her theory.

The first place she stopped was the Shuckery. She had to get that out of the way first.

Sheldon greeted her at the door. She said, "I'm not here for food, Shelly. I'm here to ask you something serious."

He made a face. "You know how I hate serious things. I would rather debone a frozen turkey. But let's step out of the doorway."

He led her to a private dining room that didn't happen to have guests at that moment.

"What is it?"

"Shelly, what did your father do for a living? And Jeanette's?"

"My father?" Whatever he had been expecting her to ask, this wasn't it. "Jeannie's father? What has that got to do with anything?"

"Humor me."

"My father was a steelworker in Detroit," he said. "He was a good provider. You know the type. I loved him, but we drove each other nuts. 'Why you gadda be reading all dos comic books, Shelly? Why you gadda be writing in dat notebook all da time?' When he found out that I was going to Paris he about had a heart attack! But it was even worse when I told him I was gonna cook. 'Don't do dat, dat's women's work,' he said. My own father."

"And Jeanette? What about her father?"

"He was a butcher, a Paris butcher. He didn't mind that she wanted to stop trying to write so she could cook. But he tried to throw a cleaver into my head when I told him we were going back to the States to do it. I don't think he liked me. Or anybody who was American."

"Did Lance Mitchell do something that made you leave the writing profession?"

Sheldon paused for a second, then said, "I think you could say that he was the straw that broke the camel's back. I wasn't that great a writer, but nobody wants to hear it quite like that. I won't repeat what he said. It's not meant for a lady's ears. Let alone yours." And then he cackled. "Ah, that S.O.B. I was surprised to hear he was coming to the island. I thought, 'You know what the best revenge would be? To get all his crew eating over at my restaurant. I don't know if he'd have the guts to walk through my door. No hard feelings, right? Until it came time to foot the bill. And then I woulda really stuck it to him!"

He laughed again.

"Too bad the S.O.B. died before I could put the entire film crew's tab on his credit card. It woulda been a pleasure to see his expression."

"Are either you or Jeanette sick? Have any infections?"

"What?" he asked, drawing out the word.

"I'll tell you in a moment. I have to make sure of something. It's to get Mickey and Jo out of jail."

He shook his head. "Those crazy kids. Okay, I'll bite. Neither one of us is sick or has an infection. I have bad knees. Jeanette, though, she's always perfection. She's gonna live a hundred years."

"Are either of you allergic to anything?"

"Not that we know of."

"So, would you say that you had plans to rip Lance off if he ever came to the restaurant, and at the very least were trying to get his film crew to abandon Nonatum's."

"I would, if that's what it took to get the twins out of jail."

"How did Jeanette feel about your plan?"

"She thinks I'm just about the pettiest man she's ever seen," he said contentedly. "'Get over it,' she says. Then I tell her that I'll get over it when he has to sign the bill." He rubbed his hands together. "What happened to him was a shame. He didn't deserve to die. He wasn't a monster, just one more jerk in a nice suit. And in a way, I have to thank him. It was only through him that I found my true calling and the love of my life. Don't get me wrong, though, I'm not going to shed a tear."

Angie bit her bottom lip, trying to think of what else she could ask. She couldn't say, "Can you prove that you didn't inject any of the cupcakes with penicillin when you visited the set to pass out lobster roll samples on Saturday?" He would say that he hadn't but that he couldn't prove it.

"Did Jeanette come with you on Saturday to the film set?"

"No. She was supervising some new trainees. We're getting them up to speed before the season starts."

"Did you notice how many cupcakes were left in the box when you were there?"

"Nope! It didn't matter, because the box was taped shut and had a note on top: *Save for Mr. Mitchell.*"

Angie blinked. They'd saved the cupcakes for him specifically?

"Did he arrive when you were there, by any chance?"

"No. I would have done something to embarrass him if he had! And you would have heard about *that* by now, I guarantee it."

She paused. She'd have to check on when Lance had arrived, whether it was Saturday evening or Sunday morning.

Because she was now almost sure that someone had tampered with the cupcakes that she had brought with her, not the ones that Mickey had sold to Lance Mitchell directly from the bakery. He had taken Sunday cupcakes with him from the bakery, then eaten those. Then he had stress-eaten all the leftovers from Saturday and the penicillin-tainted one had finally caught up to him.

After all, Mariam had remembered seeing *two* boxes of cupcakes in his room on Sunday night when she had brought him a cup of Earl Gray tea. And Lance had only taken away a single box of cupcakes with him on Sunday. If she remembered correctly, Mickey had mentioned at some point that Lance had only bought a half-dozen cupcakes from the store.

As anyone who has ever stress-eaten before knows, you can pack away an *amazing* amount of food once you get started eating. She had brought about a dozen cupcakes with her in the box on Saturday. Some of the Saturday batch must have still been uneaten on Sunday night. A stress-eater with a sweet tooth could put a dozen or more cupcakes away in a single day.

"Earth to Angie," Sheldon said.

She startled.

"You looked like you were having a moment there," he said, "but I should get back to the floor. Did you get what you needed?"

"Yes, thank you," she said.

"Jeannie and I in the clear?" he said, obviously joking. He even winked at her.

"Yup! Totally," she said.

"Glad to hear it. Good luck!"

"Thanks." She shook off her thoughtful mood. She had more stops to make before she could talk to Detective Bailey, and she wanted to get this over with as soon as possible.

Next up: Al Petrillo.

Al Petrillo was staying at the other cottage at the Island Harmony B&B along with the director and a few other people. She drove to the B&B and parked next to one of the VW Microbuses. The evening was chillier than usual, but at least she had dressed warmly before setting out.

She threaded her way across the big yard where weddings were often held, around the cottage that held her store's books, and over to the cottage with the climbing roses, where the others were staying. She knocked at the door, which was already cracked open.

"Come in!"

She stepped inside. The cottage was hot and brightly lit. A bunch of the crew, including people who stayed at the other B&B and the hotels around town, were sitting around in the chairs and couches in the living room, drinking coffee and discussing where to go out to eat.

"Hello, bookstore lady," Jim Urban called out. "How's it going? We're just about out of coffee. Did you bring some?"

"As it happens, I did," she said. "I thought about you guys for some reason. Can I have someone help me bring it in from the car?"

Jim Urban jumped up, as did a gaffer that Angie vaguely identified as being Jo's boyfriend Teddy's friend on the set—Jo had shown her a picture of the two of them while they had all been complaining about Lance Mitchell on Sunday night.

"It's not locked," she called to them. "Where's Al? I have more books for him."

"Upstairs," chorused several voices.

"That guy goes through more pulp than a sawmill," Sandra Potvin commented.

"He's just a speed-reader, like me," Angie said.

The director said, "It's better to take your time on books. To savor them slowly and deliciously."

"Books?" Sandra asked sarcastically. "Chocolate, maybe. But not books."

"I thought you liked to read?" Angie asked.

"It's okay," Sandra said. "I'd rather do something real, though. Something that leads to results. Changes lives, etc. You know."

The director turned to her. "That's a strange opinion for someone who works in movies."

"I provide an injection of sanity," she said.

"Sometimes the best people are a little bit nuts, though," Angie said.

"It's an entire industry full of narcissists, sociopaths, and Machiavellian types," Sandra said. "A little balance isn't a bad thing."

"True." Angie tilted her head to the side, mulling this over. "Hey, I don't hear any footsteps upstairs. Am I safe to go knock on his door? Which room is he in?"

They told her, and she climbed the stairs. Behind her, she heard Jim and the gaffer come in with the coffee pots.

Angie walked up the stairs. The top of the cottage had creaking, painted wood floors covered with thick, friendly rugs. She knocked on Al's door.

"It's me, your friendly book delivery service," she said.

"Come in."

She opened the door. Al was lying on his stomach on the tiny, quilt-covered twin bed, propped up on his elbows reading a book.

"I didn't send you an email," he said. "It must be something good."

She closed the door behind her.

"Al, I just needed an excuse to ask you some questions."

"Yeah, okay," he said. "But did you bring me any books? What's in the bag?"

She handed it over.

"*Misery,* by Stephen King," he said. "And...*Gone Girl. Double Indemnity. The Maltese Falcon.* I've read all these." He frowned at her and put a scrap of paper in the book he'd been reading, setting it to the side as he sat up. "What do you need to ask?"

"The box of cupcakes that was on the set on Saturday. Did you see anyone eating any of them?"

He shook his head. "The box was all taped up. I didn't *see* anyone. I heard that Julia ate one. Lucy Smith saw her and freaked out. 'You're on a diet! Don't touch those!' I thought she was going to lose her mind. I presume she was the one who taped it shut and put the note on top."

Angie said, "Were you hired on this project because of or in spite of Lance Mitchell?"

"Because of," Al said. "He was harsh about my work as a director, but he's always liked me as a camera operator or director of photography. He has never said so in public, though. If I got too successful, I might not be as easy to hire."

"Why was he working on this project?" Angie asked. "I thought he was more successful than this. Why would he work on a cheesy TV movie like this?"

Al shrugged. "Someone called in a favor."

"Who?"

He shook his head. "I don't know. But they got Julia and Rob both signed up, too."

"Does Rob have any connection to Lance? What's the backstory there?"

"None that I know of. But his stuntman used to be his lawn guy."

"Really?" Now, there was something interesting.

"Yeah, Lance caught the guy doing flips into his pool to cool off and set him and Rob up together."

"You make it sound like they're dating."

Al laughed and said that wasn't the case. "But sometimes you can be closer to your stunt double than you can to your girlfriend."

"Is Rob seeing anyone?"

"No."

"Jim?"

"Yeah. He and Sandra Potvin have been dating for a couple of weeks.

Or, I should say, friends with benefits, more than anything else. They're both kind of casual."

"Do you know her well?"

"Kinda. She's Julia's sister, you know?"

"I heard that," Angie said carefully, continuing on. "They're both such beautiful women. Their parents must have been actors, too."

Al laughed. "You'd think so! But Julia's mom and dad are farmers," Angie remembered Julia mentioning her parents' avocado trees. It still surprised her that a celebrated Hollywood actress came from such humble beginnings. "Anyways... Julia's dad isn't that great looking, but her mom, whew! She's a looker. That's where both girls got it from."

"It sounds like Sandra has a different father," Angie said.

"Yeah, sorry. I'm used to calling them both sisters, but they aren't. They're half-sisters. I don't know Sandra's dad. He was out of the picture before I met them. Sandra doesn't talk about him much. I got the feeling that he was a politician or something in France. Whatever he was, he was highly respected."

Angie nodded and said, "This might be coming out of left field, but were you and Sandra *together* at one point?"

"Uh..." he said. "I guess that's the word for it."

"Oh. Got it," Angie said. "More of friends with benefits situation?"

"Right. But I did get to go to the farm once. Met their mom. Farm's not that far from L.A." He paused. "You think Lucy Smith did it, don't you? That's why you're asking about Sandra and Julia? And it's why you loaded me up with femme fatale books? *Misery*. She's Julia's biggest fan, you know? It's kinda weird, the way that chick is so obsessed with Julia."

Angie said, "Please don't say anything to anyone. I don't want anyone else to get hurt. The less anyone knows about it, the better."

"Gotcha."

"I should go now before someone gets suspicious."

"We were talking about stories, that was all."

She smiled at him. She had a feeling that it looked a little thin and stretched. "We were. A murder mystery, as a matter of fact."

Julia Withers was not at the cottage. A casual inquiry got her the information from Sandra Potvin that she was still at Jellicoe House with Lucy Smith.

"How did she seem?" Angie asked. "Is she feeling any better?"

Sandra looked frustrated. "I can't tell. One minute she seems like she's soldiering on. The next she's a mess and the only thing keeping her from crying her eyes out is Lucy going on and on saying don't wreck your make-up. The hold that guy had over her was scary, even when he was alive. She needs to get over it."

Angie frowned. "I'm sorry to ask such an intrusive question, but..." She looked around the room. "Um. Can I ask you outside?"

"Sure," Sandra said, pushing herself up.

Angie and Sandra walked outside, standing away from the door.

"What is it?" Sandra asked.

"I need to know if Lance had something blackmail-worthy hanging over your sister's head," she said.

"You think that's why he was killed?"

Angie said, "I think it might be."

"Julia didn't do it."

Angie bit her lip. Thinking quickly, she said, "It was Lucy who taped up the box of cupcakes on Saturday, wasn't it?"

Sandra turned to the side of the cottage and put her arm against the shingles. "Lucy? It was Lucy who took that bastard down?"

"I think it's very likely, yes."

"I almost want to thank her. Why would she do it?"

"You know that she's protective of Julia," Angie said. "Lance may have pushed Julia too far, but Lucy was the one who snapped."

Sandra nodded. "I should have seen that. She's like a cross between a bodyguard and a mother hen. That's one intense lady."

"No kidding. I can't prove anything, though," Angie said. "The police might have evidence, but I'm still on the edge."

"You're going to tell them, though, right? You're not just going to wait around?"

"No."

"Good. I mean, I said that I almost want to thank her, but it's not right."

"I'm sure there are a lot of people who would rather this was all swept under the rug," Angie said.

"Like Lucy." Sandra turned back toward her. "I'm assuming that you're going to go talk to her next."

"I need to talk to Julia," Angie said. "But I think I'm going to avoid talking to Lucy as much as possible. Detective Bailey can do that. I mean, I'm not a complete nut."

"Do you want me to come with you?"

Angie thought about it. "I don't know. Wouldn't that make Lucy suspicious?"

"No, I've been checking on Julia a lot. To make sure she's okay."

"I don't really have an excuse to be over there," Angie said. "Why don't we call her and go out to eat somewhere? Or has everyone eaten already?"

"We all ate," Sandra said. "It's three hours later here."

"They were talking about where to go to eat inside just a moment ago."

Sandra chuckled to herself. "Well, yeah. They're greedy."

Angie chewed the inside of her cheek. How could she get Julia by herself? She didn't want to try to ask her questions in front of Lucy Smith *or* Sandra Potvin. "Maybe I'll ask her tomorrow."

"It'll be fine," Sandra said. As if reading Angie's mind, she said, "You can talk to her privately. I don't need to snoop. It's about when she was having sex with Lance, isn't it? Like, was she sleeping with him lately and who else she was sleeping with. That kind of thing."

Angie felt her face heat up. "Yes."

Sandra laughed. "You're so obvious. Come on, let's take your car.

Those vans are great, but they stick out like a sore thumb. The press is still parked near the building hoping to get a scoop."

Before they left, Angie told the others that she and Sandra were going to Jellicoe House to check up on Julia. She added, "And if you still haven't figured out where to go for second supper and drinks, I recommend Sheldon's Shuckery. The drivers will know where that is."

"That's what it was called!" Jim said, beaming. "The guy that brought the samples. Good stuff. Thanks, bookstore lady."

Angie could totally picture the guy mowing lawns and taking breaks in rich people's swimming pools. "Trust me, it's great. I highly recommend it."

## Chapter 15

## UNDER SURVEILLANCE

Jellicoe House, not being the kind of place where guests indulged in raucous evening entertainments, was settling down for the night when Angie pulled up into the parking lot. Several white vans with satellite dishes were parked there as well, decorated with news station logos.

What would it be like to live like this? Constantly under surveillance?

It would make her skin crawl.

Lucy Smith's bedroom window was still lit. So was the window next to it. Julia's room.

"I don't think she'll hurt Julia," Sandra said. "But I'd still like to be sure."

"Me too," Angie said.

"We need to find a way to separate them. Then we can call that detective."

"I'm thinking about calling him now," Angie admitted.

"I'd feel better if we waited until we were sure Julia was safe."

That was the real reason that Sandra had come along with her, Angie realized. She would do almost anything to protect her sister.

"Any ideas?" Angie asked.

"We could come up with something that Julia needs desperately and ask Lucy to get it for her."

"That might work," Angie said.

"Will you be okay if I leave you alone with her? With Lucy?"

"I don't think she knows that I suspect her," Angie said. The hair was standing up on her arms. "I should be safe. Let's do this." She twisted around in the seat and grabbed the canvas bag holding the books that she'd been meaning to bring to Jellicoe House after telling Mariam that she would. "Um. What do I do if the news crews try to talk to me?"

"They won't," Sandra said. "You don't look that interesting. They're after a movie star, not a normal person."

"Thanks, I guess."

Angie let herself out of her car, pulling the books after her. Sandra got out. They passed the three news vans quickly.

"Don't you want to lock your doors?" Sandra said.

"Why would I?" Angie asked. "Nobody breaks into beaters like this when it's not tourist season."

Sandra laughed, though it sounded a little strained. She was stressing out about this as much as Angie was, apparently. "Nobody on the island steals things? I find that hard to believe."

"There's nothing in the car worth stealing, including the car itself. What are they going to do, disguise the car and try to smuggle it off the island?"

"Geeze. This seems like the kind of place where people don't even lock their front doors," Sandra said.

Angie shrugged. "We trust each other here."

The two women walked up to the front door, where they were met by Mariam. "Oh, good," she said. "I'm glad to see you, Sandra. Your sister is losing her mind again. Did Lucy call you?"

"I had a feeling she had worked herself up again," Sandra said, her tone serious. "She's a sensitive soul."

Mariam winked at Angie. "And you're here as moral support, I see."

"Yes, ma'am. I also remembered that I had a bag of books for Jellicoe House in the back of the car."

"What do we owe you?"

"Look the books over first. I would rather spend the extra time now getting the right books for your business than chasing a fast buck."

Mariam made an approving noise and accepted the bag of books. "I'll let Mrs. Keene know. She'll be pleased."

Angie and Sandra went upstairs to Julia's room. They could hear the sobbing from the stairs.

Angie knocked. "Julia? Are you all right?"

The sobbing didn't stop, but footsteps came to the door. It opened a crack. Lucy Smith peered out at them.

Her face was completely flat and expressionless. "What is it?"

Angie stared at her. Her mind had gone completely blank. What could she say that would make Lucy open the door and let them in, but that wouldn't give away what she wanted to do?

Sandra said, "I had a feeling that she was upset. Angie happened to be over at the cottage to talk to Al, so I asked her to drive me over here, so the paparazzi wouldn't bust us."

Lucy closed her eyes for a moment. In a low voice, she said, "I don't understand why this is so hard for her. Shouldn't this be a weight off her shoulders? Shouldn't she feel relieved?"

"Maybe she feels guilty about feeling relieved," Angie suggested.

Lucy sighed. "I feel like actresses should understand their feelings better than this."

"Actresses," Sandra said, "only need to be able to express their feelings, not understand them. But they do have to look pretty doing it."

Lucy shook her head, then let them both into the room.

Julia was curled up in a ball and pressed against the wall next to her bed. She had pulled off the quilt and wrapped herself tightly. Even her head was covered.

Sandra crossed the room and put her hand on her sister's shoulder. "Julia? It's Sandra."

"Why won't you all just go away and leave me alone?"

"I don't care what you look like. And I *don't* care if you smeared your makeup. I'm sorry that I teased you about it earlier."

"You said I looked like a goth pig."

"I was mad at you because you're still crying over that jerk. He didn't deserve you and you know it."

Julia's only response was to cry harder.

"I'm sorry," Sandra said. "I'll stop being mean about him, okay? The important part to me is that you're upset and hurt, and I want to comfort you however I can. Being sarcastic and mean is, like, my comfort zone, okay? So, I'm sorry I said that. I'll do something else."

"Thank you," came a small voice.

"Come over here and sit with me," Sandra said. "I'm starting to feel like you don't even like me, the way you're all the way over against the wall like that."

Julia turned over on her other side, the quilt flopping over with a thump, then scooted slowly toward her sister.

Angie turned to Lucy. "Um. Maybe we should leave the two of them alone for a while. Maybe that would help."

Lucy stared at Sandra, a twisted look on her face as Sandra rubbed her sister's shoulder, making comforting noises. It was strange watching such a tough-looking woman be so gentle.

"We can wait downstairs in the lobby and make sure nobody comes up to bother them," Angie added.

Lucy walked out of the open door that Angie was holding for her. The two of them walked downstairs and found Mariam standing behind the desk.

"The back door is locked, isn't it?" Lucy asked Mariam.

"Yes, did you need it open?"

"No, I just wanted to make sure the press couldn't try to sneak in while we were downstairs."

Mariam clucked her tongue. "You're just about worn out by now, I would think. Would you care for a cup of chamomile?"

"I have a feeling that I'm going to be up for a while," Lucy said. "How about some Earl Gray?"

"Certainly." Mariam disappeared into the kitchen off the main reception area.

The two of them walked to a pair of overstuffed chairs near the front door. Lucy took the one that would allow her to watch the front door.

Angie wasn't sure how to handle this. She had been able to separate Lucy from Sandra and Julia. Or rather Sandra had separated them. Should she excuse herself and make the call to Detective Bailey now? She couldn't do it in front of Lucy, of course.

Rather than sitting down, Angie said, "Will you excuse me for a moment? I need to make a call."

Lucy grabbed onto Angie's wrist. Tears were streaming down her face. "You can't go outside. The press will see you. They'll know why you're here."

Angie bit the inside of her cheek.

The press didn't know who she was and hadn't bothered either her or Sandra when they had come in. But Lucy's nerves were so shredded that she wasn't thinking straight. Which, as far as Angie was concerned, was a good thing.

Angie decided to give her a moment to cool down before she made the call.

"Are you okay?" Angie asked. "Mariam was right. You look like you're about one last straw away from a nervous breakdown."

"I feel like I'm trying to defend someone under a microscope by throwing my body in front of the lens," Lucy said. "No, even better. I feel like I'm trying to save someone who's a complete idiot about love, from herself, while *she's* under a microscope."

"That sounds about right," Angie said.

"Has there been any progress on the murder investigation?" Lucy asked.

Feeling like she was walking on a bit of a tightrope, Angie glanced toward the front desk. Mariam hadn't returned yet.

"Not really," Angie said.

"You know something," Lucy accused her.

Angie shook her head. "Nothing important. Stupid rumors."

"Who do you think did it?" Lucy bared her teeth in a grimace. "Why can't this all go away? It's not like Lance Mitchell was worth it."

Angie pressed her lips together. Fortunately, just then Mariam came out of the kitchen with a silver tray with three mugs on it. She sat next to them in a third chair, curling her legs up underneath her.

"Well, loves," she said. "Whatever it is you're talking about can't be good. You look like you're about to spit nails at each other. Are you sure whatever it is can't wait until after you've both had a good night's sleep?"

Angie said, "I should probably wait for Sandra to come back down."

"That might be all night. I can tell her to give you a call if she needs a ride. Or I can drive her back to the hotel she's staying at later. We'll sneak ourselves right out the back door and take my car. The honorable press need not know that she's even left."

Angie hesitated, then made up her mind. "Okay. But give me a moment. I need to make a call."

A thump came from upstairs.

Lucy jumped off her chair. "What was that?" In a flash she pounded up the stairs. Mariam and Angie looked at each other, then both stood up. Mariam went up the stairs, Angie right behind her. Lucy had entered Julia's room.

Julia sat on the edge of her bed with her hands over her mouth. Her quilt had come partially unwrapped, showing a beautiful woman dressed in a ratty t-shirt and sweats, makeup smeared and hair tangled into a damp rat's nest against her neck.

Sandra was holding a cell phone. She glared at Lucy.

"I called the police," she said to Angie. "They're on their way to arrest the killer."

"The police?" Mariam asked. "Why? What's wrong? Are you all right, Miss Julia?"

Julia's face remained a horrified expression, fixed on one spot. Mariam turned to see where Julia was looking.

At Lucy.

Mariam's eyes widened, and her face drew back, going pale.

"You don't mean..."

Sandra said, "Don't say it. Not now."

Angie took a deep breath. She was shaking. She hadn't expected Sandra to be the one to call. "Let's...sit down."

"What's going on?" Lucy demanded.

"Like you don't know," Sandra snapped.

Angie knew that if she didn't step in, things were going to get ugly very quickly. She took two steps forward and put herself between Lucy and Sandra. Sharply, trying to copy Aunt Margery's sternest tone, she said, "Stop. Both of you. Sit *down*."

Sandra took a step backward, sitting on the edge of the bed next to Julia. She tossed the phone down on the sheets.

Again, Lucy said, "What's going on? Why is she looking at me like that?"

Julia's voice seemed to emerge from the far corner of the room. She sounded small, weak, and terrified. "Because you killed Lance."

"What!"

"Don't try to deny it," Sandra said. "Even Angie has it all worked out. The cupcake that killed Lance Mitchell was in that box that Angie brought to the set. *You* were the one who freaked out and taped it up after Julia tried to eat one. *You* are the one who's obsessed with Julia. How many times have you said that you'd do anything to keep her from getting hurt? Angie heard you threaten to hurt anyone who messed with her. I heard it too. At the bookstore. You're crazy, Lucy. I pity you, but you're dangerous."

Lucy turned toward Angie with a dismayed look on her face. "You think I'm crazy?"

Angie had no idea how to answer that. "Let's just wait until the police get here."

"Seriously? You're just going to let them arrest me? Is this some kind of a joke?"

"No joke," Angie said.

"I can't believe this. You can't possibly have any real proof. Just this stupid guesswork." She took a step toward Angie. "I didn't even—"

Angie cut her off, saying coldly, "Stay right there."

"What do you think I'm going to do, hurt you?"

"Let's just all stay put until the police get here."

In the distance, they could hear sirens approaching. Angie tried to keep her face looking stern. When really, she was shaking like a leaf. She hoped none of the others noticed, although that was probably too much to ask for.

"This isn't fair!"

"You'll get a lawyer," Angie said.

They were lucky that the other guests were at the Island Harmony cottage, for the most part. At least nobody else would get mixed up in this.

Sandra stood up. "Julia and I are getting out of here. The rest of you can wait for the police. But it will break Julia if she has to face this right now."

Lucy's shoulders slumped. "Oh, God." She put her hand over her face and started sobbing.

Sandra pulled Julia to her feet, holding the blanket over her shoulders.

"Aren't you going to stop them?" Mariam asked, looking to Angie. "Aren't we all supposed to wait for the police?"

Angie shook her head. "It's better this way. Otherwise someone might get hurt."

Sandra and Julia walked around the side of the room away from Lucy. Not that Lucy would have noticed a herd of elephants running through the room at that moment. She had realized that the best thing she could do for Julia was let her go.

Angie almost felt sorry for her. She dug in her pocket and handed Sandra her keys. "Go back to that beach we were at the other night and wait for me. I'll get one of the officers to drop me off when this is done."

"Got it," Sandra said. "I think I can get there. I'll take Julia out the back door, then drive around and pick her up. If we're lucky, nobody will know we're not here."

The two of them left down the other end of the hallway, the back stairs creaking, then the sound of a door spring slowly stretching before softly closing.

The sirens were closer now. Almost there.

"Why did you do it?" Mariam asked Lucy in a horrified whisper.

"She didn't," Angie said.

Chapter 16

# THE SOLUTION WAS IN A BOOK

The women heard Angie's car sputtering to life, the sound only discernible to someone who'd been driving it for years. Angie held up a finger to silence Mariam. Lucy was still sobbing to herself.

The car pulled slowly through the gravel parking lot. The passenger door—it had its own special creak that Angie recognized—opened, then slammed. Then opened and slammed again. Julia must have gotten the quilt stuck in the door.

A moment later, the car drove the rest of the way through the gravel lot, then pulled out onto the road.

"Good," she said. "That's them out of the way, unless a police officer tries to chase them."

"What are you talking about?" Mariam asked. "What's going on?"

Angie didn't answer. She was waiting for the sounds of sirens.

Which, about two minutes later, pulled up to the front of the B&B. Angie breathed a sigh of relief.

Julia was perfectly safe. Sandra wouldn't hurt her. Angie didn't think she would be a danger to anyone else, either, unless someone threatened her. She just didn't care enough about anyone else to bother with hurting them. Her sarcasm was cutting enough.

Mariam said, "Angie. Don't make me call your great-aunt."

"Sorry," she said. "I didn't know what else to do. I had to get rid of her. And she won't hurt her sister."

"What are you trying to say?" Mariam asked.

"Sandra is the murderer."

Mariam stumbled. Lucy continued to sob. She must have already guessed what was going on.

Angie put a hand gently on Lucy's arm. "I'm sorry I had to speak to you so harshly earlier. I didn't know what else to do but play along and hope that she would decide to leave."

Lucy continued to cry. Angie led her over to the bed and helped her sit down, then sat beside her.

A knock came at the door downstairs.

Mariam shook her head. "I...I'll get that." She left the room, and soon the stairs began to creak.

Angie tried to soothing Lucy, but it didn't seem to have any effect.

After some quiet words were spoken downstairs, the stairs began to creak again. Detective Bailey appeared at the open doorway of Julia's room. He knocked on the frame.

"Come in," Angie said.

"You let the murderer drive off in your car," he said.

"I couldn't think of what else to do," Angie said, for what already felt like the hundredth time. "I sent her to Nobadeer Beach."

"Yes, Mariam already said that. Some men are on their way over to the beach to pick her up. And hopefully rescue your vehicle."

"It's not much of a car," Angie said. "As long as Julia and everyone else is safe, I can be pretty happy about how everything turned out."

"Happy?" the detective asked incredulously. "You let a pretty solid suspect in a murder investigation get away with your car and a potential hostage."

"She would never hurt her sister," Angie said. "You should have seen how protective she was of her a few minutes ago."

"People don't always act rationally when they're cornered."

"They don't hurt the people they truly love, though," Angie argued. Then she flopped over backward on the bed. "I'm sorry, Detective. I really couldn't think of anything else to do that wouldn't get me or Mariam or Lucy hurt. I think she knew that I suspected her. She wouldn't leave me alone. I decided to just play along and hope for the best."

"It was dangerous."

"I know."

"Well," he said, sitting down in an overstuffed chair next to the bed. "Tell me what happened."

"After you told me it was penicillin and not cyanide, I was devastated," Angie admitted. "I had to go over everything all over again and try to look at everything from a new angle. I can't believe that you gave me that lecture on being wrong, and I was still making all kinds of stupid mistakes."

"We all make mistakes. It's what you choose to do about them that matters."

"Well, it turns out that I chose to feel like a complete idiot. So, I gathered some more information. That is, I read a book."

"The solution was in a book?"

"Well, part of it. There's a new Hollywood tell-all book that came out. It's just barely fictionalized enough to keep the author from getting sued, even though Lance Mitchell threatened to do so when he came to the bookstore and spotted it."

Angie suddenly remembered him glaring briefly at Sandra after he had come in, although she hadn't made the connection between Sandra and the book. Sandra had been the one to suggest that he try the cupcakes still in her pastry case. That's when he had glared at her. Angie could still remember how intense that look had been.

"The book is called *Delusions of Filmmaking,* and it's about a young man who goes from being a naïve director-wannabe to a major Hollywood player...who gets screwed over by even bigger Hollywood players, and ends up having to work on made-for-TV movies instead of major blockbusters."

Detective Bailey raised an eyebrow. "Sounds familiar."

"Doesn't it? The book starts out in France in the early two-thousands, in a loose circle of filmmaking students and amateurs, both French and expat Americans, who were admirers of the Nouvelle Vague filmmaking movement."

"You're joking," Detective Bailey said.

Angie realized that he hadn't read a book on the subject, and that the name of the movement *did* kind of sound weird. "No, seriously. Just take my word for it; there was one. It was in the Sixties. A bunch of people admire it."

"Well, all right. Go on."

"While the real person satirized in *Delusions of Filmmaking* was in France, he wrote a book about the Nouvelle Vague movement that became really, really famous. The book was turned into a documentary, and that became famous, too, although mostly only among film students and directors, people like that. Film buffs."

"Which I'm not."

"Me either, I'm more of a reader," Angie agreed. "But the important part is that, in *Delusions of Filmmaking*, the author stated that the main character had had a co-writer. However, before publication, the Lance Mitchell character takes all mention of the co-writer out of the book, off the copyright and the cover, and has the book published without giving credit to the co-writer. In the book, the co-writer drops out of the picture and just disappears, unable to continue in the film industry once they found out how badly they got screwed."

"Which, I think what you're saying is, where you got the motive for the crime. The sins of Lance Mitchell's past finally caught up with him."

"Sort of. But let me tell you some other things first."

"You're making my head spin already."

She grinned. "If you think this is complicated, you should try reading an Agatha Christie novel. I *also* read the book that Lance Mitchell wrote, which is called *Nouvelle Vague*, after the film movement."

"Okay. Two books. One about the film movement, another one full of nasty Hollywood gossip about fans of the film movement."

"Correct. The *Nouvelle Vague* book, the serious film movement book, mentions something interesting in a footnote."

Detective Bailey rolled his eyes. "In a footnote. You checked all the footnotes."

"It's the one place that hints at the fact that there really was a co-author. It mentions something about the author's father being a noted French chemist. Which Lance Mitchell's father was *not*."

"That's not exactly proof."

"I'm pretty sure that the author of *Delusions of Filmmaking* has some other evidence to back up her claims. That book is practically begging for someone to try to sue. It's almost as though the book was written deliberately to provoke a lawsuit, so the evidence could come out in court."

"Okay."

"*Delusions of Filmmaking* mentions an incident in France in which the main character, the Lance Mitchell lookalike, has an infection on his foot that gets treated with penicillin, after which he throws an irrational fit because he thinks his foot is going to get cut off, and he gets kicked out of the hospital. The reader finds out that the character is *extremely* allergic to penicillin, and almost dies but doesn't."

Detective Bailey said, "Now we're talking."

"It's not proof," Angie said, "but it's suggestive. The tell-all book accuses Lance of stealing credit away from a co-writer and notes that he's allergic to penicillin. The film book has a hint that a co-writer was indeed once involved in the creation of the book. And we know now that Lance died from a severe reaction to penicillin."

"Where did you get Sandra Potvin out of all of this? When you talked to me the last time, she wasn't even on your list of suspects."

Angie nodded. "I weeded all of the other suspects out. It was a mess. First, I thought that the cupcakes that I had brought to the set on Saturday should be ruled out, because someone that picky couldn't possibly eat leftover, stale cupcakes, right? Then I found out from Mariam that the box of cupcakes that he had picked up on Sunday, which had a green and pink Nantucket Bakery ribbon, and a second box, without the ribbon, were both found in his room. Both sets of cupcakes were there, from Saturday and Sunday. She said both boxes were empty, and she didn't say that she'd thrown out any cupcakes from his garbage. So, he either ate them all or gave some away."

"And he wasn't the kind to give a cupcake away. Everyone says he had the worst sweet tooth."

"That's right. When I brought the first box onto the set on Saturday, most people refused to try them, saying that I needed to save them for Lance. The only person who tried one was Julia, I found out later, but Lucy panicked and taped up the box. At any rate, I shouldn't have ruled out the first box of cupcakes. From talking to Mariam, it really did seem that nobody tampered with the cupcakes once he got them to his room."

Detective Bailey nodded slowly, processing what Angie had told him. Suddenly his cell phone rang. He held up a finger to Angie and answered it.

"Bailey. Do you have her in custody yet? No, the other one's sitting on the bed and crying her eyes out. I don't think she's going anywhere. I'm listening to Miss Prouty explain things." He grimaced. "Keep looking."

"What's the matter?" Angie said.

"They haven't found her yet," Detective Bailey said. "Neither the women nor your car were spotted at the beach."

Angie immediately pulled herself to a sitting position, then started to stand.

Detective Bailey waved her back down. "Your place isn't out on the road looking for a murder suspect. Might as well keep talking. At some point you should get to the part where you explain about your telling everyone that Ms. Smith was a suspect, only she really isn't."

"I'll get there," Angie promised. "The cupcakes."

"Yes. The cupcakes."

"I knew that Mickey hadn't poisoned them."

"You mean, you assumed he hadn't."

Angie flopped backward again, staring at the odd angles of the ceiling around the dormer windows. "I had to make some assumptions. So, I assumed that none of the second box of cupcakes, the Sunday cupcakes with the ribbon, had been injected with penicillin, because Lance hadn't shared any, and because he had taken them straight to his room. The box was empty, so he had eaten them all, and presumably would have eaten them first. Therefore, it was the first box that must have contained the culprit."

"You assumed."

"I assumed that the cupcake hadn't been tampered with at the store. Most people aren't allergic to penicillin, but some people are. Tampering with one of the cupcakes *at* the bookstore would have been a stupid risk. If someone had come down sick from a cupcake before Lance Mitchell could eat the one he was supposed to eat, then the store would have been shut down, health inspectors would have come in...the plan would have failed."

Detective Bailey grunted disapprovingly.

"I also knew that you hadn't said that the half-eaten cupcake from my store had been injected with any kind of penicillin, and you would have tested it by now. I decided that it was more likely that the cupcakes would have been tampered with on the set. Given that everyone's reaction to eating the cupcakes was so negative, the murderer could be reasonably sure that the cupcake wouldn't get eaten by anyone else."

Lucy Smith's shoulders were still shaking, but she wasn't making any sounds.

Angie said, "The reason that Lucy got so upset at the thought of Julia eating one of those cupcakes was probably that she's on a diet...and she was afraid of Julia giving Lance any excuse to start a fight."

"Yes," Lucy said. "I didn't know...I didn't know. I didn't see Sandra doing anything to the cupcakes. I only thought, *Let's head off a fight before it can start.* Better to let the cupcakes go bad. Nobody wanted to eat them. I taped them up. Lance might scream at everyone about wasting food, but he would blacklist people for eating *his* cupcakes."

"But they weren't even his," Detective Bailey said. "Nobody would have ever known."

"He would have found out," Lucy said. "He always finds out somehow. Even if Julia doesn't throw it in his face."

The stairs creaked again, a slower step. It was Mariam coming up with a tray heavy with tea. She sat the tray on an antique side table near the bed and poured it into cups.

"Have they got her yet?" she asked.

"No," Detective Bailey said.

"I wouldn't be surprised if she doesn't just disappear off the island," Mariam said. "Some way, somehow."

"I'm half inclined to agree with you," Detective Bailey said.

Angie's stomach had tensed up. She'd feel better after all of this was over, or at least when Sandra was in jail.

"Are you going to let Jo and Mickey go soon?"

"Probably. The Chamber of Commerce has been all over me to get this resolved so they can get their pastry supply secured for the summer. What we would do without pastries over the summer, I don't know." He rolled his eyes. "Far more important than justice. But go on."

"So, I suspected that the murderer had injected one of the Saturday cupcakes with penicillin, knowing that sooner or later that box would end up in Lance's room. She expected him to eat the cupcakes right away, but he didn't—or he didn't eat *all* of them in one sitting. When Lance came to the bookstore on Sunday morning to chew out everyone on the crew, Sandra told him to eat one of the cupcakes in the case, the one that he had taken a bite out of. She was the one who told him to do it."

"We should be able to get corroboration on that," Detective Bailey said. "From what I hear, there were a lot of witnesses at that point."

"She wanted him to be thinking about cupcakes. She knew that he had a sweet tooth and that he would eventually eat everything sweet he could easily get his hands on. He didn't leave his room on Sunday night for supper. He ate nothing but cupcakes all night. If she knew him well enough to write a book with him in France, she knew enough about him to know that, once he got started, he wouldn't be able to stop. Kind of like a drug addict in that respect."

"So, this all sounds like a good theory," Detective Bailey said. "But what proof do you have? What evidence do you have that I can take with me to court? We only get one real chance at this, you know."

"I'm not that far yet," Angie said. "First I had to get rid of everyone else. I finally realized that even though Lance could have made an enemy of everyone on set, he hadn't really done so. Most people don't make lifelong enemies out of their bosses over rude behavior. They grin and bear it until they can get a different job, right? Which meant that while I kept thinking that *anyone* could have killed Lance, it truly could have only been someone with a stronger motive than just getting rid of the guy with the rude behavior."

"I guess I can agree with that," Detective Bailey said.

"People who had been personally and directly hurt by Lance Mitchell were pretty much the people who I brought up earlier. Sheldon left France and became a cook because of something Lance Mitchell said, but he seemed more interested in making Lance foot the bill at the restaurant than killing the guy. He had moved on from the harsh criticism. He got the girl, the restaurant, and a successful career out of it. So, he had a hypothetical reason to murder Lance, but not a practical reason."

"Good to hear it. It would have been no end of trouble if it had been one of the two of them."

"But you would have arrested them?"

"I arrested Walter when it looked like he was the one who killed his father," Detective Bailey said. "Don't you give me the side-eye, woman."

She smiled at the ceiling. "Okay, okay. Next, Al Petrillo. He had also received some harsh criticism from Lance that ended up changing his life. But, again, it just meant that he gave up his dreams of being a writer and director and became a really sharp camera operator instead, much admired in the industry. In fact, he got a recommendation from Lance that helped him build his great reputation. So, he had even less of a motive."

"And Julia?" Detective Bailey asked.

"Julia didn't do anything," Lucy said.

They all ignored her.

Angie said, "Julia has been hurt by Lance Mitchell time and time again. Why would this time be any different? She tries to make him into a better man, but fails, every time. But let's say that something changed, and she's decided that she's done with Lance, but wants to be able to grieve for him dramatically. She knows enough about Lance to know that he's allergic to penicillin and has a fondness for sweets. She sees the cupcakes and decides to inject one of them with penicillin."

Detective Bailey screwed up one eye. "But..."

"But her assistant has been following her around the set," Angie said. "And the moment that she would have needed to inject one of the cupcakes with penicillin, she instead gets busted by her assistant for going off her diet. She couldn't alter the cupcake before Lucy taped the box shut. She couldn't alter it when it was in Lance's room. The door was locked, and she didn't have access to the keys. They don't just leave them hanging around on hooks in the open."

Mariam said, "We've had problems with guests being stalked before. By ex-husbands mostly. But we never give extra keys out, no matter how good the excuse is, if they're seeing each other or married, or even if we've had the person as a guest before. The guest with the key has to do it."

"So, Julia's out."

"Thank God," Lucy said.

"What about Lloyd Rapinski?"

"Again, we're talking about someone who has been around Lance long enough to be used to him. Why kill Lance and put himself out of a job?"

Detective Bailey said, "I got the impression that the man was about to lose his job anyway. That was why he was so anxious. What do you have to say about that?"

"Just that It would reflect badly on him if his boss died of an allergic reaction on his watch. Who'd want to hire him?"

"So you don't have any proof that he couldn't have done it?"

"Not really. But do you seriously take him for a suspect?"

"No. As it happens, we know that he was away from the set at the time the cupcakes were available for tampering. He did take the cupcakes from the set to the B&B, but the writer was in the VW Microbus with him at the time, and he gave the cupcakes to Mrs. Keene as soon as he came in, to take up to Lance's room. After that, he drove to the ferry landing to meet Mr. Mitchell when he came in."

Angie relaxed onto the bed. "Whew. I was starting to think you might have something on him."

"Just testing you. Rob Blake?"

"Doesn't have anything against Lance Mitchell."

"I'll let that stand for now," Detective Bailey said. "But I think you can guess how I feel about that as evidence in court."

She nodded.

"Lucy Smith, then."

"She was my second favorite choice, once I thought of her. Every insult that Julia ever had to stand from Lance Mitchell, she probably felt twice as bad as Julia ever had. Julia's emotions seem to come and go very quickly. But Lucy seems to hang onto things."

She felt awkward discussing this while lying on a bed next to the woman, who felt as tense as a piece of wire. But it was better to get it all out into the open. Really it was.

"But if Julia was being watched by Lucy, Lucy was being watched by Julia," Angie said. "Julia was still in love with Lance. She would have noticed anything that Lucy did against him. And I think the one thing that Lucy wanted for her boss was to have the strength to just walk away from him. Murdering Lance wouldn't have accomplished that."

Detective Bailey said, "That all sounds like a pretty strong case for murder to me."

"For a while I wasn't sure," Angie admitted. "But then I remembered her coaching Julia through confrontations. When it came to the emotional stuff, she kept coming back to the message that Julia had to learn how to cope with life instead of curl up and hide from it."

"That was your proof?" Detective Bailey asked incredulously. "That's it?"

"That was what made me look for proof. The proof was that if Lucy was watching Julia like a hawk at every possible moment, then Julia was also watching Lucy—and Julia was also watching Lance. If Lucy had tampered with the cupcakes, Julia would have noticed. Because she was obsessed with him, even if he didn't really love her."

"All I've ever wanted for her was to be able to walk away on her own two feet," Lucy said. "I knew that if I managed to break them up, she would either get back together with him...or date someone else just as bad. But she couldn't do it."

"I wouldn't feel too bad about it," Angie said, patting her on the shoulder. "I used to date a guy kind of like that. I couldn't see it either. The bad things that other people could see about him, I couldn't see, because he made sure that he kept me distracted from the bad things by accusing me of being everything I've ever been insecure about in my whole life."

Angie felt something inside her loosen. It was strange talking about Doug McConnell so casually, as if he didn't still have the power to hurt her. For a long time, she had been afraid that he would show up on the island and somehow talk her back into dating him.

Now she wasn't.

She shook her head. A weird thought, but she couldn't let it distract her.

"So now you've laid out why your suspects didn't do it," Detective Bailey said. "But you still have to tell me what kind of evidence you have that links Sandra to the crime. And don't tell me it was nothing."

Angie licked her lips and reached inside her coat, which had a big inner pocket for a phone or a computer tablet. The freezer bag she had put there crinkled. "It wasn't nothing."

**Chapter 17**

# CLOSE TO HOME

Detective Bailey's phone rang. He pulled it out and checked it, then grimaced. "Well, I'm afraid I'm going to have to interrupt our local sleuth's finest moment to answer this."

Angie had frozen in place on the bed. She had a sick feeling in her stomach. Something was wrong.

"Hello?"

Detective Bailey's eyes suddenly glanced toward Angie. "Uh-huh," he said. "Go on."

A few seconds later, he started shaking his head slowly, eyes still on Angie.

"No, I can't blame you," he said. "I'm just glad that you had second thoughts about it. Stay right where you are. Don't go anywhere. Just stay put. We'll be there soon."

He hung up, then dialed another number. He held up a finger to his lips. "*Shhh.*"

"Hello, this is Detective Bailey speaking. We have a possible hostage situation related to the arrest in the Mitchell case. It's at 1051 Quince Street. I need you to go in quiet and dark."

It was all Angie could do to keep from crying out. She found herself standing up with both hands over her mouth.

That was *her* address. The cottage. *Oh, no,* Angie thought, *Aunt Margery!*

Detective Bailey gave more instructions. All available units were to block off either end of Quince Street and deploy themselves so that they could catch anyone who tried to leave. If any vehicles, even those of the neighbors tried to leave, they were to be stopped, no matter who was driving. It seemed to go on forever. Angie's head spun.

Her red VW Golf had been spotted in the driveway. The patrolman who had spotted it knew they were looking for someone in a red Golf —but he hadn't made the connection that it was Angie's car he was supposed to be looking for.

He only saw that her car was in her driveway the way it always was.

Fortunately, he'd said something to the dispatcher, joking about what a coincidence it was that there were *two* red VW Golfs on the island. The dispatcher had lost her mind, screaming at him to call detective Bailey *immediately*.

Even in the warm B&B Angie was shivering so hard she was shaking. She felt like she was going to vomit and was doing all she could to force the feeling away. She couldn't afford to panic, not now.

She said, "I told Aunt Margery to lock the doors and not open up for anybody, but I guess she didn't listen."

"Two women drive up to your house saying that your grand-niece told them to come there to stay safe from the nasty murderer, what are you going to do? Tell them to go away?" Detective Bailey said.

Mariam still hadn't caught on. "Angie? What's going on?"

"Sandra Potvin is the killer," Angie said, "and she's at my house with Julia Withers and Aunt Margery."

"What does she want?" Mariam asked.

Detective Bailey answered her. "Dollars to donuts, she'll want a private boat to take her to the mainland. Do you have any guns at the house, Miss Angie?"

"No," Angie said. "but we have kitchen knives and things like that." Suddenly, she was angry. "Someone's going to try to put pressure on us to let her go, aren't they? The same people who pressured you into arresting Mickey and Jo."

Detective Bailey shrugged. "I prefer to think of it as protective custody. If I hadn't arrested them, what are the chances that the murderer would have killed one of them to frame them? High enough to make me worry. But let's get ourselves out to the car and on our way."

"We?" Angie asked.

"If I leave you here, what are the chances that you'll tell one of the press vans what's going on and catch a lift into town with them?"

"High enough that you're right to worry about it," Angie said.

"Then let's leave the press out of this and get moving."

~

Detective Bailey didn't turn on the cherries on the police car he was driving but he did put the pedal to the metal and turn on his flashers. In eerie silence they rushed toward Angie's home.

The entire town seemed to hold its breath. As they passed through the streets, cars were already pulled over to the sides of the road. No red and blue lights flashed. No sirens blared.

But when they pulled onto Quince Street, lights switched off, Angie counted at least a half a dozen marked and unmarked police cars parked just out of sight. No yellow tape marked the boundaries between safe and unsafe territory, it was too dangerous of a situation for that.

The officers were waiting for them.

Detective Bailey said, "Has Ms. Potvin contacted anyone to make demands yet?"

The answer was negative.

Detective Bailey stood in the glow of a streetlamp. A loud *thwack* carried across the night air as his palm made contact with his forehead. He turned to look Angie, tension etched on his face.

"Miss Prouty?" he said. "Do you have your phone turned off?"

She pulled it out of her purse to check it. She'd turned off the volume earlier, so she wouldn't be disturbed while questioning people. She normally kept it in her inner pocket, but with the freezer bag in there, she'd had to move it.

Apparently, she hadn't noticed the cell phone vibrating in her purse.

It was buzzing as she took it out. Aunt Margery's number.

She looked at Detective Bailey. He nodded. "Keep calm and agree to everything she says. Tell her whatever she wants to hear, promise her she can have whatever it is that she asks for."

Angie answered the phone. "Hello?"

Aunt Margery cleared her throat. "Well, *someone* finally decided to answer her phone," she said.

Her voice sounded far away, like the reception was bad. Angie cursed her outdated cell phone.

Then she said, "Dear, I'm in trouble. I know you told me not to let anyone into the house, but I did. Two of the women from the movie set showed at our door, both in tears, saying that you told them to come here. They said that murderer was on the loose, and that they were told they'd be safe here. Now call me a goose if you must, but it seems I now have a murderer in the house. She's asking to speak with someone who can help her get off the island."

Aunt Margery's voice sounded steady but strained, as if something was off. Angie supposed this was natural enough when a murderer was in your home.

"Let me talk to her," Angie said.

"I would think she would rather speak to the detective," Aunt Margery told her. Then she said, "All right." There was a shuffling sound.

"Hello, Angie," said Sandra Potvin. "I decided not to go to the beach after all."

"I should have realized you wouldn't," Angie said. "Is Julia okay?"

"She's fine," Sandra said. "Your Aunt Margery is trying to comfort her with a mug of hot cocoa. You don't need to worry about her. I hobbled her ankles with a belt. Something you learn how to do when you're obsessed with horses, actually. She can't move to try something stupid, so she should be fine as long as she keeps listening to what I have to say."

Angie bit her lips. "I'm glad to hear they're okay. Do you want to talk to Detective Bailey now?"

He was holding his hand out for the phone. Angie shook her head gently, and tapped the speakerphone button on her phone. Detective Bailey nodded and stood close so he could hear.

"I just have one question first," Sandra said. "Why?"

"Isn't that what I should be asking you?" Angie replied. "I guess I can see why you did it. At least I think I can. But why now? That's what I want to know. Why kill him now, after all this time? I'll trade you a truth for a truth. I'll tell you what you want to know, and you tell me what I want to know."

"Deal," Sandra said. "But first, let Detective Bailey know that I want one of the small boats we used during filming available for me in one hour. I'll meet it at the beach by Whale Rock. Tell him."

Detective Bailey nodded, and without responding, he immediately placed another call.

Angie said into the phone, "He's calling now."

"I can hear him. Why now...why now, you want to know? Why didn't I kill him sooner? Well, I had to wait until after the book came out

"*Delusions of Filmmaking?*"

"Did you like it? I'm assuming you read it. I wrote it myself. Didn't even need a ghostwriter."

"You were trying to provoke him."

"I wanted him to know that his career was going to go down in flames. I wanted him to know, as he was dying, that everyone knew who and what he truly was. Once the book was out, it was just a matter of pulling some strings to get us together on a set, somewhere away from Hollywood, preferably somewhere that would limit his coming and going. I couldn't have chosen somewhere better than Nantucket, actually. After I did some digging around the island I found out that one of your little friends had a connection to good old Lance. One mention of Jeanette and he was ready to film here." Angie could practically hear the smug sense of satisfaction in Sandra's voice.

"So, you waited until you were able to exact the perfect revenge," Angie asked. "For fifteen years, though? That's serving it pretty cold."

"He *ruined* my life. Fifteen years ago, when we worked together on *Nouvelle Vague,* I was on the verge of making it big, being known for creating something truly wonderful. And *he* took that *away* from me. He *stole* it from me. He got all the fame and glory and I was left behind to be the unknown *makeup girl* on his movie sets. I was angry and heartbroken. Maybe I could've eventually gotten over it, if I'd been able to distance myself from him. If I hadn't had to watch him and Julia continually break up and make up. I guess it takes time to realize that your sister is never going to get over the poisonous snake that wrecked your life, and that eventually, she's going to allow him to poison her too. I tried to be supportive. I tried to be there for her and to help her, but eventually the constant crying and fighting, and breaking up and running back got old." Sandra's words were almost flippant, but her voice sounded tense. "Julia was always promising to leave him for good, but then she'd go back. I knew the situation wasn't going to change, and I knew that *he* wasn't going to change. I finally decided to do something about it. He had already ruined my life. Julia and I are very different, but I love her like the sister she is. I couldn't sit back and watch him ruin Julia's life. He betrayed me, he ruined my sister, and he got what he deserved. Your turn. Why?"

"Why what?" Angie asked.

"Why didn't you just it go? He was an awful man, nobody is going to miss him. It's not your responsibility to track this down, to find me. Why did you do it?"

Angie paused to think about what her answer should be. If she told the truth, would she anger Sandra enough to make her hurt Aunt Margery?

If she lied, would Sandra be able to tell?

Probably.

"I've been asking myself that same question, Sandra, and I'm not sure I have an answer for you. I feel committed to this island, to this community to my friends and family. It was family that finally led me to you. I was looking at some old family pictures," Angie said. "That's how I figured out it was you. I started thinking about family, and then the mention of the chemist father in *Nouvelle Vague*. I realized all your connections to science, and boom. The dots were connected."

"You busted me with your *family pictures*?" Sandra asked incredulously.

"Well, I had all the facts lined up, but then I found out that cyanide was never part of the picture. I was wrong."

Now Sandra was chuckling. "I wondered how you would react to that."

"It forced me to stop and rethink everything," Angie continued, "but all I was doing was thinking myself in circles. Around and around. I was frustrated and exhausted, and then I heard some very wise words. They made me think about how similar we are to our parents. How you, the child of a chemist, must have learned a lot about science from him."

Sandra let out a chilling laugh. "Yeah, good old dad. Can't say I would have known so much about the penicillin had it not been for him. Bet you didn't know it has to be taken on an empty stomach. I had to put enough meds in that cupcake to knock out an elephant."

Angie thought she heard chatter in the background. Angie flinched, picturing her great-aunt and Julia crying out in anguish.

"Sandra, please. I want you to think carefully about what you're doing," Angie pleaded.

"Oh, you think I'm going to hurt your aunt? I won't, not over this. Of course, if the cops start shooting, someone's going to get hurt, and it isn't going to be me. I can't control that. But really. Why couldn't you just drop this? If you'd have just let it go, the cops never would have caught me in time."

"Murderers tend to think they're the good guys. They tell themselves, 'If only the other person had done things differently, I wouldn't have had to kill them.' But that's not how it works. If someone deserves justice, that should be left up to the judge and jury. Otherwise the decision is too emotional; it's personal. Nobody has the right to make that type of judgement."

Sandra's voice was sharp. "And you are objective? You trust yourself to make that kind of judgment? Turning me in isn't personal?"

"No," Angie said. "I mean, I'm *not* objective. I *don't* trust myself to make that kind of judgment. That's why I'm working with Detective Bailey. Because I can't make a judgement on something this serious."

"That's crap," Sandra said, "you're hiding behind the lawman. It's personal for you."

Angie composed herself and shot detective Bailey a glance. He met her glance and held up his notebook for Angie to read. It said *Keep her Talking*.

She nodded, and composed herself.

"Okay Sandra, maybe it is a little personal, my friends were in jail and that's motivating. Also, I hate liars. I was engaged to a guy who stole my work and passed it off as his own, did you know that?"

"So why don't you understand how much I hated Lance?"

"I do understand," Angie said. "That's just it. But I hated his lies more than I hated *him*. And I hate it when people try to pressure you into covering up their own bad judgment. I also hate that everyone in this town seems to think that they can demand that I solve this case, and then tell me I have to do it in a certain way, one that doesn't embarrass anyone."

Sandra was silent for a moment. "I guess that's an answer I can understand. Everyone tells you to hush it up. You can't deal with the hypocrisy. You have to tell someone. I get it."

Angie rolled her eyes. Sandra failed to grasp the gravity of murder, but personal slight made sense to her.

"All right, Angie. I'm going to hang up now. Don't call me again until the boat's in place."

"Don't you want to talk to Detective Bailey?"

"I think it's all under control for now," Sandra said. "Everybody stays calm and it all works out."

"Except for Lance."

Sandra gave a sinister chuckle. "I wish I could have seen the look on his face."

~

The curtains on the main floor had all been pulled. The lights were on, but it was impossible to see inside.

Detective Bailey said that the chief of police intended to go through with the deal on the boat. It was, he said, their best chance to separate Sandra from Aunt Margery. He agreed with Angie's assessment that Sandra wouldn't harm Julia—but the fact was, he pointed out, that sometimes in a hostage situation, a police officer inexperienced in hostage situations might be the one to panic. And Nantucket's police force didn't have much experience in hostage situations.

Angie struggled to keep her cool, but it wasn't easy. Her stomach was doing flip-flops.

"So, tell me while we're waiting for this boat to be prepared," Detective Bailey said, "What evidence do you have connecting Sandra Potvin to this case?"

Angie laughed. She had completely forgotten about trying to wrap up her big moment: so much for her detective story-like grand reveal.

"It seems insignificant," she said. "You're going to laugh at me."

"What?"

Angie took a breath. "I found out from Al that Julia Withers and Sandra Potvin are actually half-sisters, but I didn't make the connection that Sandra and Julia don't have the same father until I started reading Julia's Wikipedia page. They're always talking about growing up and spending holidays together. But, after I had my big ah-ha moment, I looked up famous French people with the surname Potvin. It took a little digging, but eventually I found it. There was an entry for Emmanuel Potvin, a famed French chemist, which connected Sandra to the footnote in the *Nouvelle Vague* book that Lance Mitchell wrote. That could have just been coincidence, though."

Bailey nodded at Angie. He was keeping up. She went on.

"But there were all these other little things. Like the fact that Sandra has a tattoo of a beaker – you know, what they used in science experiments. When I first saw it, I thought it was just some odd little inside joke. But she mentioned an obsession with French, loving makeup because it's like a science... All this started to add up. I figured, hey. The apple must not fall far from the tree. I guess we always carry a little piece of our parents around."

"Wow. Okay. You've really been doing your research, Angie. I have to say I'm impressed."

"There's one more thing. The pièce de résistance, if you will." Angie said, raising one eyebrow.

She pulled the freezer bag from her coat pocket. Inside was a small, charred, twisted mass of plastic that she'd picked from the ashes of the beach bonfire. The orange bottle was melted, its white cap still intact.

"What is it?"

"At the bonfire, Sandra Potvin, Al Petrillo, and I sat together around the fire. While we were talking, Sandra took a small white paper bag out of her pocket, stared at for a minute, and tossed it into the fire. I didn't give it a second thought...until after I made the family connection and suspected Sandra. On the off chance that it hadn't been totally destroyed, I checked the bonfire ashes. It was still there. It's melted, but not completely destroyed. Looks like a prescription bottle if I've ever seen one." Angie hurriedly added, "Oh, and I didn't touch it. I used the plastic bag to pick it up."

She could tell by the look on his face that she was in for a lecture on how civilians should handle evidence: they shouldn't. But done was done.

He took a deep breath, taking the freezer bag from her.

"Did you happen to see a name on this? Before it burned?"

She shook her head. "It was in a paper bag."

He went to put the evidence in the car, then returned, arms crossed over his chest staring at the house. She could almost hear him thinking, *Don't scream at her right now, her great-aunt is a hostage!*

Angie stared at him. Something about the phone call with her great-aunt was gnawing at her.

Detective Bailey felt her gaze and turned to her. "What?"

"I have a feeling that..." she started to say, then slapped herself on the head. "Is the ferry shut down?"

"I have two officers watching it, but the suspect is still in the house," he said. "I'm more worried about your great-aunt than I am about that ferry."

She cleared her throat. "How do we know for sure she's still in the house? What if she only pretended to be calling from inside? Detective Bailey, Sandra is a *makeup artist, and she does incredible voice impersonations.* Believe me, if there's anyone who could pull off a quick, completely convincing disguise...it's her."

Detective Bailey made a face, then grabbed his cell phone from his pocket to make a call. After a brief conversation, he hung up. "The ferry was just about to leave. They're searching it now."

After a full minute, Angie couldn't bear the silence any longer.

"Should we go over to the dock?"

Detective Bailey looked over at the cottage. "We're going to wait here until we hear one way or another. If she's still in the cottage, she might panic if she sees movement that she doesn't expect. And if she's at the ferry—then I don't want you in the way."

Angie made a face.

After a what seemed like an eternity, but was actually only five minutes, the Detective's phone rang. He picked up immediately and had a short, hushed conversation just out of earshot from Angie.

"Detective Bailey. Any news?" she asked.

He paused, then put a hand on top of his police car to steady himself. He shook his head.

"Nothing?" she asked, disappointed.

He cleared his throat. "Not nothing - they got her. Dressed as a middle-aged woman and wearing your great-aunt's clothing. They only caught her because the ID she gave them came out of a leather studded wallet which didn't fit the character."

"Was she using Aunt Margery's ID?"

"No. We're not sure where it came from. Probably a tourist."

"Was Julia with her?"

"Nobody spotted her. I hate to say it, but we're lucky you thought of it. If she'd been able to get over to the mainland..."

"But she didn't," Angie said. "Now, let's go save my great-aunt."

Chapter 18

# LET THEM EAT CAKE

Aunt Margery and Julia Withers had been tied up in the darkened storage-slash-guest room inside the cottage the whole time. Angie hadn't spoken to her great-aunt on the phone *at all*. It had all been Sandra, very cleverly disguising her voice. She had taken Aunt Margery's cell phone with her onto the ferry.

Sandra hadn't hurt either one of them. She had only wanted to get them out of the way. Julia had refused to cooperate with Sandra's plans to run away and had gotten in a fight with her over Lance's murder. Frustrated, and knowing that the cops were closing in on her, Sandra had finally abandoned her sister. Thankfully, Sandra had missed the earlier ferry due to her fight with Julia.

The ambulance took Aunt Margery and Julia to the hospital, not because they were hurt, but because Detective Bailey wanted an official physicians report for the trial. Angie watched the ambulance pull away, and then opened her voice mail to listen to her messages. When she focused on the sound of the voice, she could tell that it wasn't Aunt Margery speaking—but only barely. Earlier, she had been completely fooled. Sandra's impersonation of Aunt Margery was that good.

As Angie was placing her phone back in her coat pocket a car screeched to a stop in the street. Two doors slammed. Just as Angie glanced up in the direction of the pounding footsteps, she was abruptly grabbed and swung off her feet. Angie shrieked, looking down at the face of the person swinging her. Turned out that Mickey and Jo had been released, finally, and Mickey had just literally swept Angie off her feet.

After three dizzying spins, he put her down, leaning his forehead against hers for a moment. "Thank you," he said, before letting go.

Jo, not as long-legged as Mickey, and therefore not quite as quick, suddenly slammed into Angie, wrapping her in a hug so tight that made Angie's ribs ache.

"Ow," Angie complained as she laughed. Jo let up a little.

Mickey said, "Is Aunt Margery okay?"

Slightly dizzy, Angie said, "Yes, she's fine! And we caught the bad guy. It turned out to be Sandra."

"I always knew it was her," Mickey said. "Who was she, anyway? I don't think I ever met her."

"Long story," Angie said.

Jo gave Angie a fiercely proud look, but said, "You sure took your time getting us out of jail."

"I had trouble figuring it out. Some people are great liars," Angie said.

"Which you hate."

"Which I hate," Angie agreed.

Mickey said, "And the bakery? Is everything okay with the bakery?"

"I haven't checked it out, but it didn't burn down or anything."

The twins looked at each other.

"Okay, we got out of jail in one piece," Jo said, "so I think that means we're doing that thing we talked about where we buy the coffee roaster and start roasting our own coffee."

"And not just for Angie," Mickey said. "Although, yes, she *is* the real reason."

Jo stuck her hand out and Mickey shook it. Clearly, they had talked this over while they were sitting in jail.

Mickey said, "Angie, you'll start buying your beans from us, right?"

"Absolutely."

"And you'll stop stressing out about what Lance Mitchell said to you if I stop stressing about it too, right?"

"If I have to."

"And you'll meet me for dinner to talk it over?"

"Sure. Now that things have calmed down the three of us should have a night at Sheldon's like old times."

Mickey paused and shot a glance to Jo, who rolled her eyes.

"Just ask her," Jo said with a smile.

"I was thinking it could be just the two of us for dinner," said Mickey.

"Mickey, are you... are you asking me out on a date?" Angie asked as a grin spread across her face.

"Yeah, Angie, I am. I know it's a little bit complicated but sitting in a jail cell for a few days makes you think about what's important, and for me, that's you. "

Angie was surprised. She certainly had feelings for him too, but Jo was her best friend. "Mickey, I..."

"Don't answer now. Just think about it. I'm not going anywhere." Mickey put his hand on her shoulder gently, and smiled.

Before Angie could say anything, a policeman ran over to her and spoke briskly.

"Ma'am. House is clear now, still a crime scene, but if you need to grab some of your belongings I can walk you through and you can pack a bag. You'll need to find somewhere to stay for a while."

"Uh, sure, that would be great. I'll come with you now."

"I'll wait for you here. You're staying with me." Jo said definitively, not a question but a statement, "and Margery is already at my Mom's house, so you better grab a bag for her too."

When Angie returned, Jo was waiting for her, and Mickey had left.

They took Margery's overnight bag over to Dory Jerritt's. As soon as they walked through the front door, Angie rushed over to her great-aunt, pausing to look her over. "Are you okay, Aunt Margery?"

"Oh, I think I'll be okay, dear. You know the old saying, 'If you are going through hell, keep going,' don't you?" she said with a wink. Her feet were propped up on an ottoman, a huge glass of red wine in one hand, and a dish of dark chocolate in the other. Yeah, Aunt Margery was going to be just fine.

Angie left with Jo, feeling a sense of calm wash over her for the first time in a long while.

The film crew wrapped things up quickly. Julia seemed to have pulled on some type of invincible emotional armor. If Angie had had to guess about her emotional state—she was back to delivering coffee to the set in the mornings—she would have said that Julia was...angry.

At her sister or at Angie, she couldn't tell. Neither Julia nor Lucy were talking to her. Or, really, to anybody.

Filming wrapped up ahead of schedule.

The books came back, neatly packed in their boxes. The director showed up at the bookstore to personally thank Angie and Aunt Margery for the selection of books. Pictures were taken as Carol Brightwell and Angie shook hands with the director.

Life appeared to be returning back to normal for Angie's small island town.

Detective Bailey called two days later. "The forensics people in Boston were able to reconstruct the label on the bottle of liquid penicillin."

Angie sighed in relief. "And? Did it belong to Sandra?"

"It belonged to a colleague of hers in L.A., a makeup artist who noticed it missing from the fridge on one of the sets they both worked on. And even better yet, we found a hair that had been caught inside the cap of the bottle. It belonged to Sandra."

"Will that be enough?"

"It's not enough on its own, but we have a good case."

"Good. Detective Bailey, can I ask you a question? Off the record?"

"Shoot."

"Was the person who pressured you into arresting Mickey and Jo presumably a person with a great deal of influence on the island, perhaps someone named Walter Snuock?"

Detective Bailey didn't answer her. "I didn't speak to the individual involved, Miss Angie, and can neither confirm nor deny."

It had occurred to her that it was Walter who was pressuring the Nantucket police force. It was a good thing they had broken up, or she might have dumped him for that. He probably hadn't *meant* for her two best friends to get arrested.

But he sure hadn't made sure the problem was fixed, either.

The evening after the last day of filming they had a farewell party at Sheldon's Shuckery, in which great praises were sung over Sheldon and Jeanette's cooking. Julia had been dragged out for the party by Lucy. She hadn't wanted to come. She'd wanted to stay in her room and cry until it was time to take the ferry back over to the mainland. Huge tears ran down her face as she tried to sit through the meal.

During the party, Al Petrillo pulled Angie to a side room where it was quieter. He handed her a plastic grocery bag with his last set of borrowed books inside. "I just wanted to thank you for delivering books."

"Not for solving the murder?" she asked archly.

He shrugged. "I figured you had about as much glory from that as you could stand."

She laughed. That was the truth. The press had tried to latch on to her. She had refused to answer any questions. *No comment* seemed to be safer than having her words thrown back in her face later. Even worse, the Chamber of Commerce had to be threatened with a lawsuit before they had been willing to remove their website article claiming that Angie had solved the case.

"Aren't we supposed to be keeping all this on the down low?" she had asked Carol. "Solve it quietly?"

"In a way, your solving the case makes the island look good," Carol had responded.

"I screwed up plenty too," Angie said.

Carol patted her hand. "Don't be modest."

It was a hopeless cause.

Angie looked at Al. "It's true. I wish people would just shut up about it. It hasn't sold a lot of books for the book store, either. It's just brought us a lot of gossip."

"You should write a book about it."

She rolled her eyes. "No. Just...no. But you're welcome, for delivering books while you were here, that is. Did you get them all read?"

He had, and he gave her a big check to cover his tab. Far more than the books had been worth—but a fair price for the boredom she'd saved him from, he said. She thanked him, and he gave her an awkward hug.

Back in the dining room, it was time to bring out the dessert—*the* dessert, the one that would be the Shuckery's summer showstopper. Mickey was standing at the front of the room, dressed in a ridiculous orange and yellow plaid suit.

"And now, for the grand finale!" he said. The tables had been cleared of dinner and everyone was anticipating Mickey's delicious new creation.

Behind him, Jo wheeled out a trolley. The silver trays it carried were covered, adding to the suspense.

With a flourish, Mickey turned toward the trolley, grabbed the domed cover off the highest tray and raised it overhead. Even Angie had no idea what he had finally come up with. He had been thinking it over constantly while he was in prison.

On the tray was a huge rounded cake.

Angie looked at it more closely and realized, that while it looked like a cake, it was baked in a swirl pattern of the most intricate fashion with beautiful layers of white frosting. It looked like a giant cinnamon bun, and the smell of cinnamon transported Angie back to her childhood.

"I give you," Mickey announced, "The cinnamon bun cake, with divine maple walnut frosting and essence of cinnamon. This is a cinnamon bun too decadent for breakfast."

Mickey caught Angie's eye and smiled as he revealed the cake. She was touched. He knew she loved cinnamon buns. Everyone clapped, and dug into the cake as soon as slices were passed around.

Angie took a bite of the cake, savoring the sweet flavors of the cinnamon and light, airy frosting that tasted like walnuts and maple syrup mixed with heaven. Mickey walked around shaking hands of guests and sharing the story of his creation with guests.

"What do you think of the cake?" he said as he approached Angie's table.

"Mickey, it's incredible, one of your best. This is so good, but I hope you didn't decide on this because of me?"

"No. Yes... I don't know. Maybe, but a good baker is an artist, and an artist needs his inspiration." Mickey grinned at her, and Angie felt herself blush.

Standing behind him, Sheldon was grinning from ear to ear, knowing that this was a successful evening that he didn't have to cook. The look on the face of the restaurant's chef was one of pure delight. Angie wondered to herself if there was a partnership brewing there. If this might just end up being more than a one-time thing.

Julia hadn't touched her plate, and Lucy encouraged her to try a bite. Julia took a deep breath, screwed up her face, and placed a tiny piece in her mouth, as though she were a kid being forced to eat vegetables.

Angie watched Julia's dramatics and realized that she was glad Hollywood was leaving the island. She would miss some of the characters - Al for sure, and even Julia to certain extent - but she was excited about the prospect of having the bookstore back to herself. Just her, her regulars, and the tourists. Some people might prefer the excitement of Los Angeles, but Angie loved her hometown for what it was; A peaceful, beautiful place. Nantucket was, and always would be, home.

Mickey continued to work the room, smiling his contagious smile and confidently cracking jokes with everyone as they finished up their desserts.

He made his way over to Angie's table and squeezed her hand again, then went to help pass around seconds. She watched him, her face hot, thinking *I've known this man forever. So why do I feel like we've just met?*

# THANK YOU!

Thank you so much for reading The Bun Also Rises! Just like baking the perfect cake, the process of publishing this book required inspired prose chefs, delightful literary ingredients and lots of patience. It was not quite easy as pie but we feel that the final product really takes the cake. We hope you agree.

Books with reviews sell like hotcakes so we'd love it if you would be kind enough to take two minutes right now to leave a review of the book. To leave a review simply visit the **book page on Amazon** and click the button that says *Write a Customer Review*.

The Bun Also Rises is book 3 of the Angie Prouty Nantucket Mysteries. Hungry for more? Be sure to check out book 1, **Crime and Nourishment**, and book 2, **Prize and Prejudice**, from Amazon today.

Thank you for joining us on this adventure!

- The Team Behind Miranda Sweet

## ABOUT THE AUTHOR

Miranda Sweet is a collaboration of authors, writers, editors, creatives, and cozy-mystery lovers. Miranda Sweet novels can be relied upon for classic cozy themes, settings and characters. Her books are best enjoyed with a hot beverage and a pastry.

To learn more about Miranda Sweet and get free books and recipes visit **MirandaSweet.com**